ABE AND THE WILD RIVER

Edith McCall

Royal Fireworks Press

Unionville, New York

Royal Fireworks Press
First Avenue, PO Box 399
Unionville, NY 10988-0399
(914) 726-4444
FAX: (914) 726-3824

email: rfpress@frontiernet.net

ISBN: 0-88092-439-X

Printed in the United States of America using vegetable-based inks
on acid-free, recycled paper by the Royal Fireworks Printing Co. of
Unionville, New York.

A NOTE FROM THE AUTHOR

Abe and the Wild River is an adventure story based on real events. Travel back in time nearly two hundred years to December, 1811, when it begins—a time when there were only seventeen states in the United States of America, and they were all east of the Mississippi River. The only American towns in all of the land west of the Mississippi were three or four villages along that river. The largest was a small fur-trading village named St. Louis.

By 1800, Americans with pioneering spirit were already going west to take wild land close to St. Louis, the "far West" at that time. Leading them was the old Kentucky pioneer Daniel Boone. The land was then under Spanish law, but Boone got the government to give him a land grant near St. Louis. To get his family and relatives moved from Kentucky, Boone's sons cut down a big cottonwood tree back in Kentucky and hollowed out the trunk to make a giant canoe, sixty feet long. Down the Ohio, up the Mississippi to St. Louis and a short distance up the Missouri came the Boone family and others, the first of many Americans to move the frontier toward the vast land beyond the Mississippi River.

When our story begins, in 1811, old Daniel Boone was still alive, living in the house one of his sons built—a house people can visit today. St. Louis was still small enough for anyone to walk its mile of riverbank and the six short blocks inland. The riverfront where the canoes, flatboats and keelboats arrived and departed was the most important part of the town. That is where we meet Abraham

Benjamin Carson, the restless fourteen–year–old son in the blacksmith's family.

The main cargo boats on the Mississippi were keelboats and flatboats. Flatboats could go downriver, but couldn't be moved much against the strong river currents; keelboats could take a cargo of furs and other products all the way to New Orleans and come back with supplies needed upriver. Steamboats were in use on the eastern rivers in 1811, but none had as yet come down the Ohio River to the Mississippi. Young Abe Carson thinks working on a keelboat would be a great adventure, a way to see the world beyond little St. Louis.

What happens to Abe in *Abe and the Wild River* is based on the historical event known as the New Madrid Earthquakes, the most terrifying conditions ever experienced on the Mississippi River. The series of quakes began on Monday, December 16, 1811, at about two in the dark of morning and lasted several months. They are still the most severe earthquakes on record in all of North America. So strong was that opening shock that it rang church bells in Richmond, Virginia, 850 miles away, awakening alarmed citizens! Based on the great distances that tremors were felt, scientists today measure the three strongest shocks, on the Richter Scale, at 8.6 (December 16, 1811), 8.4 (December 23, 1811), and 8.7 (February 7, 1812). The epicenter was very close to the Mississippi's west bank, south of St. Louis, in Missouri's "boot heel."

We know exactly what happened on board a real keelboat caught in the start of that December 16 major shock, because John Bradbury, an educated man from Scotland, wrote in his journal of the horrors of that night. His notes reported the details of what took place on the keelboat on which he was then traveling down the river. As I told the story of *Abe and the Wild River,* Bradbury's notes, plus recorded interviews with people who lived in the little cabin settlements nearby were my guides. All that Abe experienced on his river journey is based on that information, which left clear pictures of the terrifying events.

Waves formed on the usually gentle Mississippi like those in an ocean storm, and for a short time the river's direction of flow was reversed. In the turbulence, the waters of the river spread so far off the old river bed that shallow Reelfoot Lake was created on what had been dry land in western Tennessee. The lake is still there today. Trees were torn from the ground and tossed about, and wild animals as well as human beings were terrorized. The earth itself roared and every living being cried out in response.

As in Bradbury's account, all on board the keelboat *Rosalie,* including the cabin boy, were suddenly jolted awake to a world of crashing uprooted trees and the horrifying shrieks of frightened wild creatures. Every board and beam of the boat creaked and groaned as the craft was tossed on great waves never before known on the quiet Mississippi. In a heartbeat it had become a raging, unpredictable wild river.

Read on—

CHAPTER 1

Action on the Levee

Abe Carson was suddenly wide awake. He had almost dozed off that early December afternoon as he sat watching the Mississippi River move lazily along. There were still some stumps, left from ancient trees, on the St. Louis levee, and he had made himself comfortable leaning against one of them. There hadn't been a single boat coming in to the landing or leaving it for the hour he'd been sitting there, and he'd grown sleepy. But he jumped to his feet as he heard a call from out on the river.

"Down on 'em, men! Move her on in!"

A large keelboat, the very best kind of riverboat in that year of 1811, was slowly making its way upriver from the south. Abe could see the boatmen working with their long "setting poles" to force the keelboat through the dark swirls of water that hindered the approach to the landing. The man on the cabin roof—the one holding the long pole that Abe knew guided the rudder board on the end in the water— would be the captain. He was shouting orders to his crew as they struggled to get the boat to the landing.

Now that he was fourteen and had learned all the village school could teach him, Abe felt he should be earning money. Since the school term had ended, he'd hoped to get a job on a riverboat—sometimes a boy was hired to help the cook or clean cabins, if the boat carried passengers. He had applied to several captains whose boats had arrived in the little fur trading village of St. Louis. So far, he'd

1

had no luck. The answer was always the same. "You're too small. Can't use a kid like you. It takes a strong man to move a keelboat against Old Man River!"

Abe wasn't looking for a job as a boatman—he knew he wasn't ready for that. So with a hopeful tone he would say, "Thought you might need a cabin boy, sir." A cabin boy's job didn't include the hard work of moving the boat along.

The keelboat coming in was bigger than many. Its cabin was long enough to carry passengers. Maybe Abe's luck would change! He walked down the sloping levee to be close at hand as the keelboat came in for the landing. Even if he already had a cabin boy, the captain of this boat might want someone to do errands or help unload as soon as they docked. The boat was so close now that he could read the name painted on the planks of the bow—*Rosalie*.

"Easy now—let 'er drift in," the captain called as he lifted the long rudder pole from the water and laid it on the cabin roof. As he stood erect, he looked toward the shore and saw Abe. He called out, "Hey, boy! Want to earn two bits?"

Abe felt a stir of excitement. "Yes, sir!" he shouted. "Sure do!"

The *Rosalie* came close to the boat landing. A big boatman, wearing a bandanna tied around his head, a red flannel shirt, and skin-tight woolen pants above laced up moccasins, stood ready to make the boat secure. He held a coiled rope in one hand. Looking at Abe, he called out, "Catch the line, kid!"

2

The rope end sailed through the air. Abe reached for it just in time to catch it.

"Hold us tight!" the boatman said, and Abe pulled until the pointed prow of the boat was close to the water's edge. A moment later, the man had leaped from the boat to the levee and stood beside Abe.

"Good work, kid. They call me Barney. What's your moniker?" He thrust a big hand out to Abe, who almost let go the line in his haste to shake hands.

"Abraham Carson—Abe for short," he said, and felt his hand squeezed so hard it hurt. He was glad when Barney took the rope from him and wound it about a short post set into the hard-packed ground a few feet above the water's edge. Barney eased the pull on the boat enough so that the prow was about five feet out into the water. On board the boat, another crew member laid a wide plank from the forward deck to the shore.

In the meantime, the captain, taller and more slender than Barney, had descended the ladder from the roof to the deck. He waited as one of the crew members came out from a doorway that led to the cabin interior and carried two carpetbags ashore. Another boatman with a small trunk hoisted on his back followed from the cabin, and both men started up the levee.

"All ready for landing, Monsieur and Mademoiselle Lagrande," the captain called. A well dressed gentleman and a girl of twelve or thirteen came out to the deck. The captain, dressed in a short, dark blue coat above pants and boots like Barney's, preceded them down the plank and turned to offer a guiding hand. The gentleman, dressed in the stylish breeches and coat that marked him as a city man, turned and took his daughter's hand to steady her.

"A pleasant voyage, *mon capitaine*. *Merci*," the gentleman said when they were safely on the levee.

"Thank you, sir. Likely we'll be startin' back to New Orleans in about a week. I'll send a message to you at Colonel Chouteau's residence in plenty of time."

The man and his daughter started up the sloping levee. Abe couldn't take his eyes off the girl. For a moment, her sparkling dark eyes had met his as she stepped off the plank, but she had looked down quickly. Now he could see only the back of her blue velvet bonnet and her matching coat that reached to her ankles, above dainty black slippers—not at all like the clothes Abe's sisters and the other St. Louis village girls wore.

He turned as he felt the captain's hand laid on his shoulder and heard him say, "You the boy who wants a job?"

"Yes sir, Mr. Captain, I'd sure like to earn some money," Abe said. He stood as tall as he could, but he had to tilt his head back to look the tall, muscular captain in the eye. His voice was eager as he asked, "Want me to help unload?"

But the captain's gray-blue eyes had a questioning look.

"No, lad. My men will do that, and besides, you don't look big enough to handle that job."

"I'll do whatever you want, sir," Abe said, pulling off his knitted cap.

But the captain shook his head. "What I need is a good strong boy to guard the boat," he said. "We're goin' up

4

to the inn for an hour or so. My men want to do a bit of celebrating, this bein' the end of our last trip up from New Orleans before the ice sets in."

"I can guard the boat, sir," Abe said. He shifted from one foot to the other, a bit uncomfortable as the captain seemed to be measuring him from his tousled, thick blonde hair to his worn leather boots.

"Unnh." The captain's grunt didn't sound encouraging to Abe. There was a moment of silence while the captain pulled off his cap and ran his fingers through his graying brown hair. "Don't know as you're big enough to handle the job of keepin' anyone off my *Rosalie.*"

"Here comes a really big 'un, Cap'n!" Barney called out. He had been busy securing the keelboat with a second line from the stern to an old tree stump on the levee. "Don't look like he's in no hurry to go nowhere. Maybe he'd like the job."

Gus Perkins, sixteen and a foot taller than Abe, was ambling down the sloping, hard-packed levee at his usual pace. At school, everyone knew that Gus never moved any faster than he was forced to. The only time he'd been seen moving rapidly was when the smaller boys played a trick on him with a bit of gunpowder on a wick they'd lit just behind him.

Abe touched the sleeve of the captain's jacket. "I'd do a good job of guarding your boat, sir. I promise."

After a quick glance at Gus, the captain turned back to Abe. A pleading look on his face, Abe pushed aside an unruly lock of sun-bleached hair. The captain sized up the boy's stocky figure and then looked back at Gus. He said to Abe, "Maybe some other time, lad, but right now I need someone closer to man size. Got valuable cargo on board. Don't appear to me like you could handle anyone who might try to get on board, son. Need an older fellow." And then he turned away.

Abe made one more try. "Gus is taller'n' me, but I'm just as strong as he is."

"He ain't neither, Cap'n," Gus put in. "I could lick Abe with my hands tied behind my back. I'm man size, I am. I can handle anyone who might try to get on board. Throw 'em in the river if they tried, I would."

"All right, you're hired," the captain said. "My men and me need to get us a bit of refreshment for an hour or so before we move out the cargo. Don't let a single person get on board or I'll tan your hide proper when I get back—and you won't get paid, neither."

The seven men of the crew were all on the levee now, anxious to celebrate the end of their hard trip up from New Orleans and get some food other than the corn pone, catfish and tough wild turkey meat they'd been living on.

Abe watched as Gus strutted up the plank to the boat deck. He pulled off his knit cap as he went. His red-brown hair stood on end.

"Rooster!" Abe muttered. "Even looks like one." He watched as Gus settled himself comfortably on a coil of rope.

"Might's well run along now like a good little boy, Abie." Gus called out. "We don't need no help from a runt like you."

6

Abe's fists were clenched as he walked away, pretending not to hear Gus's taunting voice. It had happened again. Just because he was short, no one would give him a chance to show what he could do. He knew he was strong—he could split firewood as well as his father.

"It's not fair," he muttered. "I'd guard that boat better 'n Gus. Likely as not, he'll fall asleep sitting there on that pile of line, 'n let someone stumble right over him afore he'd wake up."

He headed upriver, walking slowly along the levee. There were a few empty barrels and a coil of rope on the paving stones in the center of the two mile long riverfront that marked Laclede's Landing. To his left he could see up Market Street to the first cross street, Rue Royale, which the American government wanted to rename Main Street. Abe thought the French name, still used by the fur traders, was much prettier.

A breeze from the southwest brought the stench for which St. Louis was well known. It came from the log buildings where the odorous bundles of pelts of beaver, bear, fox, raccoon, or silky otter were stored, most of them awaiting shipment to the main trading company shops and offices at New Orleans. Often the village boys and girls held their noses and pretended they were about to be sick when they went by those warehouses.

Abe turned up Market Street, where the captain and his crew had gone, to see if he could find work at one of the shops, or maybe at the Chouteau mansion where the two passengers were going to stay. The big stone Chouteau house faced Rue Royale. As he reached that street, Abe saw a two-wheeled cart coming, pulled by a donkey led by

7

a woman. From her appearance, Abe knew she was one of the many French-speaking villagers, in town to sell some of the potatoes she had stored from last summer's garden patch.

If I had something to sell, I could make some money, Abe thought. He had helped a little with his family's garden last summer, but the Carsons, Abe's father, mother, and two sisters, had just enough vegetables left to carry the five of them through the winter. Abraham was oldest of the three children.

"Pommes de terre! Pommes de terre!" the French woman called out, and the housekeeper from the big cut-limestone house where Auguste Chouteau and his family lived came hurrying out, carrying an empty basket for the potatoes she would buy.

Everyone in town knew how Auguste Chouteau, now a distinguished gentleman of sixty-two years, had come up the Mississippi from New Orleans with Pierre Laclede in 1763, before there was a St. Louis. Auguste was only thirteen then, but Laclede had trusted him to lay out the streets and direct the building of the first houses of St. Louis the next year. Now Chouteau was at the head of the city government and an important fur-trading business.

Abe watched while the Chouteau housekeeper bought a basketful of potatoes and then hurried over to her. Here was his chance to ask about work at the mansion.

The housekeeper spoke little English, but she understood Abe's question. Shaking her head, she said, "No, no. *Demain, demain.* You come back."

Abe smiled, and said, "I'll be here in the morning!" He might have work tomorrow! And maybe he might see the girl who had come on the keelboat. She and her father must be inside the big house now. Whistling, he turned back down Market Street to the levee.

The levee wasn't this quiet very often. A few boats were docked along this part of the riverfront—some canoes, a boxy Mackinaw boat like a flatboat with pointed ends, and a small keelboat that had arrived on Wednesday. It brought glass and nails and cast iron hardware from Pittsburgh, Pennsylvania. Usually there were shouting boatmen around, most of them calling to each other in French. Abe sat down on a log and gazed out over the river, glancing down at the newly arrived keelboat now and then. No one was around, so Gus was having an easy time of it.

"Pretty soft! He's making money just taking a nap," Abe muttered. "I'll bet if I went back down there and got on that boat, he wouldn't even hear me. Prob'ly sound asleep."

Just then he heard singing coming from up the river. "French fur traders coming back," he said aloud. He jumped to his feet and hurried down the levee. He could see the boat coming from the north, from the Missouri River. It was the kind of boat the French traders often used—two hollowed out log canoes, called *pirogues,* with a platform built between them. It was loaded with bundles of pelts.

The happy French *voyageurs,* as the traveling traders were called, sang and shouted all the way to the landing. Where Abe had been alone on the levee a few minutes earlier, men and boys arrived as if by magic to greet the travelers.

Two men came down from one of Chouteau's warehouses to help the returned voyageurs unload the cargo and carry the hundred–pound bundles up to the warehouse. Abe watched for a few minutes, until, out of the corner of his eye, he saw a rough-looking man leave the crowd and head toward the docked *Rosalie*. Abe decided he'd follow to see how Gus handled the situation.

He pretended to be just strolling along, about fifteen feet behind the man he was following. Even from that distance, he smelled bad. His greasy-looking buckskin pants, moccasins and shirt looked as if he'd slept in them for months.

Sure enough, the man headed for the keelboat gangplank. Abe stood still, about ten feet behind him, waiting to see what the fellow would do. He saw that Gus was now stretched out on the rope coil, and snoring loudly enough to be heard even these twenty feet away. *Just as I thought—he's sound asleep!*

The man stood for a moment at the foot of the gangplank, obviously making his plans and checking out the sleeping guard. He coughed. No response. Then he said, in a low voice, "Hey, you on board—" Gus continued to snore from his comfortable nest on the coil of rope. His long legs hung over the rope and his arms were crossed on his chest. He didn't move as the man began a cautious start up the plank.

Abe tensed. *What should I do? I have to stop this man from getting on board.* As the fellow took a second

10

cautious step along the plank, Abe ran quickly forward, and threw himself onto the ground. With his arms reaching out over the water, he grabbed the plank and tilted it just enough to make the stranger lose his balance.

"Hey!" was all the man had time to cry out. He waved his arms wildly and the next moment was thrashing about in the water of the great Mississippi.

Gus was on his feet now, blinking his half-asleep eyes at the stranger in the water, and trying to grasp the situation. Abe was also back on his feet, standing on the plank. He turned and looked up the levee as he heard the keelboat captain's voice. The captain and Barney were hurrying toward the *Rosalie*.

"What's going on here?" the captain shouted. The would-be intruder was now some twenty feet down the river, trying to climb onto the levee.

Gus grinned. "I told you I wouldn't let no one get on board, cap'n," he said. "Sure stopped that fellow—threw him in the river like I said I would."

Abe could hardly believe his ears—Gus sure had nerve!

CHAPTER 2

An Important Friend

His face red with anger, the captain stood, hands on hips, staring at Gus. As the silence lengthened, Gus's grin faded, and he moved about uneasily, trying to escape that steady gaze.

Then he straightened up and was his usual confident self again. "You saw him in the water, Captain." The captain's lips tightened. Gus didn't sound quite as confident as he added, "I stopped him, didn't I?"

"No," the captain said. "You didn't. I saw the whole thing."

Abe stood near the gangplank, not saying a word. He jumped a bit as suddenly the captain's hand gripped his left shoulder and squeezed it hard. "This lad dumped him into the river while you slept. Now get off my boat and be quick about it!"

Gus' hands dropped to his sides as he walked down the plank. He stopped in front of the captain and thrust his right hand out as he said, "I want my pay, like you said, Captain."

"I don't pay anyone for napping on my boat. Now move on before I help you along!" The captain raised his foot threateningly. For once Gus walked fast, moving on up the levee. Abe was about to leave, too, when the captain said, "What did you say your name is?"

"Abraham Benjamin Carson, sir. Abe for short."

"I'm Captain Byrne, Abraham. I saw you dump that fellow into the river and I thank you. You may be short on height, but not on brains. Wait here a minute." He went on board the boat as he spoke and disappeared into the cabin.

Barney had been watching and listening. As the captain left, he came close to Abe. "Good work," he said. "I'll let you in on somep'n, Abe, but don't let on to the cap'n that I told you." He paused. His gray eyes seemed to be seeing all the way through Abe's blue ones, into the boy's mind. Then, apparently satisfied, he went on. "Our cabin boy left the boat down at Saint Genevieve—wanted to get on home, and we're gonna need a new boy for our trip back to New Orleans. Should I put in a word for you with Cap'n Byrne?"

Abe's eyes widened. *New Orleans! That is the big city where Uncle Daniel's family lives...*he gulped. "Sure! You think the captain might let me hire on?"

"Well, sure! What else would I mean?"

The captain was coming from the boat's cabin, carrying a canvas sack, which he held out to Abe. "Here's the mail sack. Take it on up to Colonel Easton, Abe, and here's a bit for your trouble." He placed a Spanish "bit" in Abe's palm. Abe looked at the pie-shaped piece of a Spanish dollar which was cut into eight pieces, and still widely used for money along the Mississippi.

By the time Abe could stammer his thanks, the captain was halfway up the gangplank, a grunt indicated he had heard, but he didn't look back.

The boy's heart was beating so fast as he climbed the levee to head for the post office that he could hardly breathe, and in his mind he was already on the way to New Orleans. The only chance he'd had so far to get work was to be apprenticed to the new barber in St. Louis. But cutting hair, shaving men, and fixing wigs was not his idea of what he wanted to do all his life, even though the barber often did some "doctor work," too—bleeding sick people, or slapping those awful looking leeches on them to pull out the illness. Being a boatman would be much more interesting, and he'd get to see far away places. Maybe he could get started as a cabin boy. Even if he didn't grow much taller, he could become stronger if he worked at it, and be a regular boatman, like Barney.

Yes, I'd like to work on the Rosalie, he decided. *It's a nice boat, clean looking and large enough to carry passengers, such as the French gentleman and his daughter.* All the way up to the post office, his mind was on the exciting prospect.

The post office was several blocks away from the river, in the new stone house Colonel Rufus Easton had built. The colonel had been postmaster for three years, St. Louis' first one. Being postmaster in 1811 didn't take much time, as mail arrived perhaps once in two weeks. The colonel's main business was as a lawyer and Attorney-General for the Territory of Louisiana.

Abe opened the door to the little room that was set aside for post office business, and pulled on a cord strung from a door frame. A bell rang in another room, and a girl a few years younger than Abe came into the post office.

14

"Hello, Mary," Abe said. "I've got the mail sack from New Orleans. Captain Byrne from the *Rosalie* asked me to bring it up." Abe felt a new sense of importance as handed the sack to Mary Easton. "Tell your father I brought it, please."

"Oh, good," Mary said. "I'll sort it out and put up the list. Father has someone in his law office right now."

Abe watched as she took the mail sack and emptied it onto the shelf behind the small window where people came to do post office business. On a wall next to the door was a large slate on which was written a list of names of people for whom mail was waiting to be picked up. There was no delivery service.

"See any mail for Carson, Mary?" Abe asked. He had already checked the list on the wall.

Mary shuffled through the letters. "No, Abe. I don't see any—"

Just then Postmaster Easton came into the room. He nodded to Abe and asked, "Is my assistant taking care of you?"

"Sure is," Abe said, "except she couldn't find any mail for Carson. But that's all right. I came because Captain Byrne hired me to bring the mail sack up from the *Rosalie.*"

Colonel Easton had been glancing through the stack of mail. "Glad to hear the *Rosalie* got in before the weather blocks the river." He pulled some pieces of mail from the pile and said, "Say, Abe, you can do an errand for me if you have time." He picked up a packet wrapped in oilskin. "Auguste Chouteau would appreciate your taking this one to him, I'm sure. Looks kind of important."

Abe took the packet and turned to go. "He'll have it in a few minutes!"

But Colonel Easton called him back. "Not quite so fast, Abe. Here's another piece for Colonel Chouteau—his Gazette." He had unfolded the newspaper and was reading the front page. "Listen to this, Abe. Mr. Robert Fulton's had another steamboat built, up at Pittsburgh. This one is the first one for the Ohio and Mississippi Rivers. She's huge—biggest boat ever seen on the Ohio or the Mississippi!" He paused to scan the column. "Says here that she's already started down the Ohio. She's stalled now up at Louisville, waiting for the rains to deepen the river enough to get her over the falls without damaging her."

Abe was wide-eyed. "Is that steamboat comin' here, Colonel Easton?"

The postmaster held onto the paper, reading more of the news. "Don't think so, Abe. Boat's named the *New Orleans* and that's where she's heading. She'll just turn on south when she leaves the Ohio. She better get going soon, before the ice comes."

Colonel Easton was folding the paper now, and shaking his head over the news. "Great things, those steamboats Mr. Fulton's been building. But it'll be a mighty long time before one of them fights its way up the Mississippi this far! Just ask any of the keelboat captains. They know the current makes the work harder than any puff of steam could manage!"

Then, at last he passed the paper to Abe, who was soon on his way back to Market Street and on to Rue Royale. He knocked on the side door of the big two story stone house where Colonel Chouteau lived. After he'd knocked again, louder, the housekeeper opened the door.

She recognized Abe immediately, and shook her head. "No, I tell you once already. No work *aujourd'hui. Demain* we have work for you."

"I know," Abe said. "I should come back tomorrow. But I have a letter and a paper for Colonel Chouteau. Postmaster Easton sent me." He held out the mail, but hardly knew when the housekeeper took it from him, as the girl from the keelboat appeared at the housekeeper's side.

"Le garçon du bateau!" she said and smiled at "the boy from the boat." Abe was tongue-tied for a moment, held speechless by the girl's warm smile and sparkling dark brown eyes—so dark they looked almost black.

"Uh—yes, ma'am," he finally said.

"Merci beaucoup." The housekeeper took the papers. "I give to Monsieur Chouteau. Do not go yet." Then she said something in French to the girl, who turned and in a moment was back with a small tart which she held out to Abe. *"Pour vous,"* she said, and dazzled Abe again with her smile.

Abe took the offered tart, and stammered a word of thanks. The door closed. He stood there a moment before he turned away and headed for home, munching the cherry tart as he went, but scarcely tasting it as he was lost in thought about that smile and those eyes.

That evening, as his family sat at supper, Abe told them about the events at the riverfront and how he'd earned a little money—and a delicious French pastry. His sister Hannah was especially interested when he told of Gus Perkins falling asleep on the job.

"I hate that big old Gus," she said. "He's always chasing the girls at school. One day he put a dead snake in the girls' outhouse." She shuddered, thinking of it and then went on. "Served him right to get caught sleeping!"

Hannah had just turned thirteen. Rachel, eleven, nodded agreement and added, "He's real mean. He keeps grabbing the rope when we want to play jump rope."

Abe said, "Yeah—but Papa, there's more news." He turned toward his father. "It was in the New Orleans paper that I delivered to Colonel Chouteau's house after I went to the post office. There's a great big steamboat coming down the Ohio River, going all the way from Pittsburgh to New Orleans."

Mr. Carson said, "Yes, I heard some talk about that at the smithy. Couple of gents from the East were talking about it while I was shoeing their horses. First steamboat seen west of the Hudson River! They said this boat is bigger than Fulton's eastern steamboats, and larger than any keelboat."

"Did they say how big?" Abe asked.

"One hundred fifty feet long—she looks like an ocean ship."

Abe tried to picture how big that would be—nearly twice as long as the big keelboat, the *Rosalie*. His thoughts turned then to Barney's exciting information about the keelboat's return to New Orleans and the job possibility.

After a moment he said, "Papa, maybe I can get work on a boat—not the steamboat, but a keelboat. There's one in port now that's real nice. If I could get to be its cabin boy, I'd earn some money, and I'd get to see other places, like New Orleans. Would you let me take the job if I got a chance?"

Mr. Carson was a big, brawny man, as he had to be for blacksmith work. Hearing the suppressed excitement in Abe's voice, he glanced quickly at his son. But he went right on eating his stew. After a minute or two, while Abe fidgeted uneasily waiting for an answer, Mr. Carson put down his spoon and leaned back in his chair. "Well, Abe, I'd really like to send you back East for more schooling, but I can't afford it. You've got a good head on your shoulders and you could do something a lot better than running a smithy like I do. Don't know as working on a boat is the right work for you either."

"Why not, Papa?"

"For one thing, you're not big enough."

There it was again! "A cabin boy doesn't have to be big like the crew," he said.

"For another thing, Abe, I'd like you to be an important man, one people look up to because you are smart. But for now, what about that chance you had to be apprenticed to the new barber?"

"Oh, Pop, I don't want to be a barber! Please say I can go on a boat if I get a chance! Maybe I could even find work in New Orleans, and I could live with Uncle Daniel and Aunt Mattie."

Abe's mother pushed back a strand of her blonde hair as she turned toward Abe, frowning. She said, "Oh, no, Abraham! I don't want you to be that far away from home. I'd worry about you the whole time you were gone."

Mr. Carson was busy sopping up the stew gravy on his plate with a thick piece of fresh bread. His wife baked bread twice a week. When he finished he said, "Now learning law is more what I'd like to see you do, son. You and Colonel Easton seem to get along well. Maybe he might take you on to study law under him in a year or two. What do you think of that idea?"

Abe liked the colonel, but the thought of being a lawyer didn't seem nearly as exciting as working on a boat. "I don't know, Papa." He was quiet a moment and then he added, "But then I wouldn't get to see New Orleans!"

Mr. Carson looked at his son sharply. "Got the itch to go and see the world, have you? It doesn't seem like it now, but you've got plenty of years ahead of you. You're only fourteen, and your mother is right. New Orleans is too far away."

"Much too far," Mrs. Carson said. "It takes weeks and weeks to even get a letter from there!"

Hannah said, "New Orleans! I'd love to go there. Do they ever hire girls on boats?"

"Me, too!" Rachel put in. "We could all live at Uncle Daniel's house."

Mr. Carson pushed his chair back and stood up. "Don't be foolish, girls. A boat is certainly no place for a girl to work. Both of you are staying here to help your mother until you're old enough to get married." He paused and then turned back to Abe. "We'll talk more about your plans later. Now go out and bring in some more wood to build up the fire. Going to be a hard freeze tonight."

Abe knew better than to argue with his father. He got up and went outside to the woodpile. As he stepped out into the chilly night air, the family's shaggy brown dog, Towser, rushed up to him, nuzzled his sleeve and made the low, growly sound that meant he wanted to play.

Abe reached down to pat Towser's head, "Can't play now, Towser. Gotta get plenty of wood into the house. Going to be cold, and you'd better get to your bed out in the shed."

As he loaded his arms with chunks of wood, Abe thought, *Papa'll be surprised when the captain offers me that job! Barney didn't think I was too small for it....*

⧗ ⧗ ⧗

In the morning, when he had split log chunks for firewood, filled up the woodbox by the fireplace, and fed Towser the table scraps from the day before, Abe left to see what work there was for him at the Chouteau house. He hoped to see the girl again when the housekeeper answered his ringing of the bell, but this time he was disappointed. He was put to work pulling up the last of the season's turnips from the garden in the back of the house, and then to turning over the soil so that it would

21

be ready for planting when winter ended and spring came again.

He was tired when the job was finished, but the two bits he was paid made it worthwhile. He had hoped the girl would come out while he was working, but not once had he seen her or her father, even when he went to the door and the housekeeper paid him for his work. A bit reluctantly, he turned to leave and headed for the street.

A man's voice called him back. *"Garçon!* Boy—will you do an errand for me?" It was Colonel Chouteau, waving to him from the front porch.

Abe ran back. "Yes sir, Colonel Chouteau."

"What is your name, boy?"

"Abraham Carson, sir."

"Oh, yes, the smith's boy. Abraham, please take this packet to the post office. Tell Colonel Easton to be sure it is in the first mail sack to go across the river and on to Kaskaskia." He handed the packet and some money to Abraham. "Pay the charges and keep whatever is left of the money, Abraham. And *merci.*"

So far, this was a good day—a very good day for earning money. Abe lost no time in getting to the post office. Mary was tending the office again, but she called her father in to take care of Colonel Chouteau's important mail.

When the business was taken care of, Colonel Easton said, "Abe, come back into my office for a bit. I'd like to talk to you."

Puzzled, Abe followed the colonel and was soon seated in a chair across from the lawyer at the big, paper strewn desk. After a moment, Colonel Easton said, "Your father stopped by this morning to talk to me about you. He asked me if I'd consider having you study law under me. I told him that you and I would talk about it. Do you think you might like to study law?"

Abe wasn't sure how to answer this. He thought a moment and then said, "Well, I guess maybe it's something I could do. You don't have to be tall to be a lawyer." He laughed a bit nervously.

Colonel Easton shook his head. "Not a good enough reason. I wouldn't want you to study law with me unless you were really interested. You aren't ready yet for such an important decision, so we'll let it wait for another time." He went on after a moment. "Your father also said that you had some notion about signing on as a cabin boy on a boat, but he didn't favor it. I told him I thought it was a very good idea."

"You did? Gee, thanks!"

"Any lad who is itching to see the world—or even a few miles of it away from home—isn't ready to settle down to study law." Easton pulled a cigar from a box on the desk and carefully cut the rough end with his pocket knife.

When he had the cigar lighted, he said, "Had you ever thought that even if you don't grow to six feet, you can always stand tall?"

Abe was puzzled. "I don't know what you mean."

"Even the shortest man can be big in ways that really count, if he is brave enough to follow his conscience, Abraham." He got up and took a large brown leather-bound book from one of the many bookshelves that lined the office

23

walls. He held it so that Abe could see the gold lettering on the spine.

Shakespeare's Complete Works, Abe read. On the cover, in larger gold letters was simply the name, Shakespeare.

"Our teacher made us read a play by Shakespeare," Abe said. "It was called 'The Merchant of Venice,' and there was a smart lady lawyer in it. She won the case, I guess you could say."

"Yes, Portia was an excellent lawyer. Had brains and used them and still was honest," said the colonel. "But I'd like you to learn a few lines from a different play—one called "Hamlet." A father is giving advice to his son who is about to go out into the world, like you will if you get the boat job. What he says is very wise. I'd like you to copy a few lines."

He put a sheet of paper, a quill pen, and a bottle of ink in front of Abe, and read aloud the lines:

> *This above all, to thine own self be true,*
> *And it must follow as the night the day*
> *Thou canst not then be false to any man.*

Abe carefully copied the three lines. When he had finished, Colonel Easton said, "Blot it and keep it with you, Abraham, until you know it by memory. You'll begin to understand what it means. Then, when you're on that boat trip and you have to make a choice of what to do, you'll remember what your father and mother have taught you about the right way to live—to be true to your real self."

All Abe could think of to say was, "Yes, sir. I'll try."

"Get along with you now, Abe. And when you've seen what's outside of St. Louis, and you've done some more thinking, then we'll see how you feel about studying law."

As he left the post office, Abe practically bounced along the dusty street. *If Captain Byrne offers me the job, Papa will let me go—now I'm sure of it. Papa pays attention to what Colonel Easton thinks.* Abe headed to the riverfront on the chance the captain would be there.

CHAPTER 3

Abe's Hopes Rise

When Abe saw the *Rosalie,* none of the boatmen were in sight, but he heard the sound of someone hammering.

"Is it all right if I come on board?" he called.

The hammering went on, but Captain Byrne's voice rose above the pounding and other voices. "Depends on what you want." He sounded a bit angry.

Abe almost turned away, thinking this might be a bad time to discuss getting a job. But just then the captain's large frame filled the low doorway.

"Yes?" he said in a questioning tone. Abe was about to speak when Captain Byrne went on, the angry tone gone. "Oh, it's you—the lad who dumped the no-good fellow into the river! Let's see—your name is—," the captain lifted his cap to scratch his head as he gazed at Abe.

Abe was happy to see a bit of a twinkle in the man's gray-blue eyes. Reassured, he grinned and said, "Abe, Captain. Short for Abraham Benjamin Carson, sir."

"Come aboard, short Abraham Benjamin Carson."

Abe was usually annoyed at people who pointed out his lack of height, but there was warmth in the captain's voice. He climbed the plank and followed him through the doorway and down two steps. There was a wall with a curtained opening to the right.

26

"I could use a spry young fellow to help me pick up and straighten out the papers I just dropped," the captain said. Pushing the curtain aside, he entered a small cabin, just large enough for a narrow bunk along the wall to the left and a high table about five feet long in front of the wall across from the doorway. It was obvious that the table served as a desk, and at the right hand end there was a wall cupboard. Besides a lighted oil lamp hanging from the ceiling, the only other furnishings were a trunk under the table and the high stool that the captain used at the desk. It was obvious that a sheaf of papers had just fallen to the floor from a gray-covered ledger, open but upside down on the table. Some of the loose papers were under the bunk.

"I'd be obliged, lad, if you'd get down on your knees and get those receipts and invoices for me."

"Sure thing, Captain," Abe said, and was down reaching under the low bunk. He soon had a handful of slips of paper and reached back to hand them to Captain Byrne. He said, "There's another couple 'way back in, Captain. I'll get them, but I have to stretch out flat, so 'scuse me if my feet get in your way...." As he spoke, he had stretched out on the floor, head and arms under the bunk. In a moment, he was squirming partway out. He reached the other papers back for the captain to take them. "Here you are, Captain Byrne, but there's something stuck in the boards away back in." He grunted as he strained to loosen a sheet of heavy paper from the joint where a supporting post for the bunk met the wall. As he got it loose he saw that there was some printed lettering on it and also lines

27

of handwriting. Even in the dim light under the bunk, it looked like it might be something very important.

The captain was still standing, holding the collection of papers in his hand. As Abe squirmed backward to get out from under the bunk, the Captain hastily put them on the table as he glimpsed the printed sheet that Abe was holding.

"Tarnation," he muttered, and reached quickly to take it from Abe's hand. "So that's where it was all this time—" He seemed to be talking only to himself.

On his feet again, Abe waited a moment. The captain gazed at the written matter, seeming to have forgotten Abe's presence.

"I'm glad I found it," Abe said, feeling a bit uneasy. "Must be something real important."

"Uh—yes, lad. Thanks for getting it out." He placed it face down on the table. Then he turned back to Abe. "Can you read?" His voice was gruff.

"Yes, sir."

"Did you read any of this?" He was holding the paper with the blank side toward Abe.

"No, sir. It's too dark under the bunk to read anything," Abe answered. He noticed that the captain's face, which was usually quite red, had paled. It looked almost white behind his graying whiskers. Even the weathered back of his neck looked paler as he turned to the cupboard, undid the latch and placed the sheet of paper inside.

Feeling a bit uneasy, Abe finally said, "That paper looked like something real important."

The captain seemed to be lost in thought. Then, becoming aware again of Abe, he turned back to him and said, "Yes, boy, it is important. But don't say anything about finding it. Forget you ever saw it..." His voice didn't have the hearty sound it had when Abe came into the cabin.

Abe shifted his weight from foot to foot as the captain seemed to have forgotten he was there. "Yes, sir, I'll remember...I mean, I'll forget all about it. Should I go now?"

Captain Byrne shook his head as if to wake himself up. His voice was back to normal as he said, "No—have you got a bit more time to spare, Abe?"

"Yes, sir."

"You said you can read, but can you write, too?"

"Yes, sir. Sometimes my writin's not too good, though."

"Likely it's no worse than mine. Now here's what I'd like you to do, lad." He turned the ledger right side up. "See here on this page—it's where I write the name of someone or a company who ordered goods brought up from New Orleans. I write the date of the order, written like this." He pointed to the last written line on a page of the ledger. Then he picked out one of the loose sheets of paper and showed Abe where the date was written. "Then, when I deliver the goods there's another date. Now this column over here shows the price we agreed on when he ordered it. Here is where I show how much was paid. And here's where I write the date delivered. This one was just delivered today, so I write December 2, 1811. See?"

Abe said, "Yes, sir. Do you mean you're gonna let me do some writin' in your book?"

The captain said, "Well, let's see what you can do." He looked through the papers and sorted them to find the receipts for other orders he had delivered since arriving in St. Louis. Laying one of them down in front of Abe, he added, "Now here's the pen and the bottle of ink, and here's an order for you to enter."

The pen was a goose quill with a steel point attached in place of the sharpened quill point that Abe had learned to write with in school. He had never written with a steel pen point. He picked up the pen and said, "Gee, Captain, I've never used a pen like this. At school we still had to keep sharpening the quill."

"Got this new kind in New Orleans. When it wears out, you just put on a new point. But you have to be careful on your upstrokes or the ink splatters a bit. Don't press hard."

Abe's hand was shaking a little as he dipped the pen point into the small square bottle that held black ink. Then, after finding the right line, he very carefully copied the new information from the receipt. The steel pen point made writing a little easier than the old quill, he noticed.

As he completed the line, he heard the captain grunt, but it was a grunt that sounded as if he was pleased. Handing Abe several of the papers that the boy had gathered for him, he said, "Now, Abe, here's the rest of the receipts for orders we've delivered. Go ahead and enter them in the book."

He turned to leave the little room. "You can go ahead, Abe. I need to see what those fellows are getting done out at the stern," he said and left the cabin.

Abe felt just a bit uneasy when he was left to try the work on his own. He wiped the pen point clean with the pen-wiper, a much-used piece of flannel cloth. Before dipping it in the ink bottle he picked up another receipt. It was marked "paid" and was for an order of a barrel of sugar, two bolts of cloth, some tea that had come from India to New Orleans, and miscellaneous hardware that the *Rosalie* had brought for Mr. Samuel Perry's store on Main Street.

He found the record of the order and then wrote the information in the right places. The next entry went much faster. As he blotted it, he let his mind drift a bit. *I wonder if he is still looking for a cabin boy. Will he offer me the job if I do this work well enough? Sure hope he will—*

He dipped the pen into the ink and as he held it, a drop fell from it onto the record book page. "Better pay attention to what I'm doing," he muttered and reached for the blotting paper to soak up the ink before it dried. The spot hardly showed when he'd finished, but from then on he kept his mind on his work.

The sounds of pounding at the other end of the *Rosalie* had stopped when he was making the last entry for goods delivered. A moment later the captain returned.

"I'm just finishing, sir," Abe said. "I hope I did it right." He waited while the captain checked the pages on which he had been working.

"Looks good, Abe. Sit down there on the bunk. Want to talk to you a bit."

31

Abe felt a sudden prickly feeling on his face. He waited while Captain Byrne seated himself on the stool by the table.

"How old are you, lad?"

"Turned fourteen this month, sir."

"Humph—don't look more'n twelve. Still going to school?"

"No, sir. I finished all the teacher could give us this term. I'm trying to find work now." Abe hoped the next word from the captain would be an offer of the cabin boy job.

But the captain just grunted. He reached into his pocket and pulled out a leather pouch from which he took a Spanish bit. "Come back day after tomorrow. I'll have you write down the goods we are taking downriver."

As he handed Abe the money, the boy felt as if the captain was looking right through him. A bit embarrassed, he turned to leave and said, "Thanks, Captain. I'll see you Wednesday morning, sir." Again, the captain's reply was a grunt.

Abe was just stepping out onto the deck when he heard the captain call, "Abe! What's your father's name?"

"John Carson, sir. He has the smithy south on Barn Street, near Chouteau's Pond."

From the deck, Abe heard the captain's now familiar grunt. As he walked down the gangplank, the sound of pounding began again and he looked toward the stern. There was the big man called Barney, on his knees, hammering a nail into one of the cleats of the running board, the narrow length of deck alongside the cabin.

"Hello, Mr. Barney," Abe called.

Barney looked up, a pleased grin on his face. "Hello yourself, Abe. Captain said you were doin' some writin' work for him. Zat so?"

"Yes, sir. Got it all done for today. He wants me to do some more on Wednesday."

"You didn't say nothin' to him about needin' a cabin boy for our downriver voyage, did you?"

"No, Mr. Barney. But he didn't say anything about it, either. Just asked me some questions."

"I'm not surprised. He's kind of close-mouthed."

Abe waited, hoping that Barney would say that the captain was going to want him for the job. But Barney had a couple of nails gripped with his teeth and could only grunt. He took one of them and put it in place to pound into a cleat. The pounding continued and Abe turned away to head up the hill.

⧗ ⧗ ⧗

As the family was finishing supper that evening, Mr. Carson pushed back his chair and then said, "Abraham, do you know a Captain Byrne?"

"Yes, sir. He's the owner of the boat I was telling you about—the one where Gus Perkins fell asleep on the job of guarding it."

Hannah tittered. "I still think he must have looked awful funny when he found out that you had dumped the man into the water." She and Rachel looked at each other and in a moment both were giggling.

Mrs. Carson frowned and said, "Girls, your father was talking to Abraham. Don't interrupt!"

Mr. Carson asked, "Have you seen the captain since that day?"

"Yes, sir. I did some work for him today. He asked me to make some entries in his record book."

Mr. Carson looked surprised. "Funny that he didn't say anything about that. He came to the smithy while I was shoeing a horse and just asked if I had a son named Abraham."

"Didn't he say anything about me working for him?"

"No. He just kind of grunted. Then I had to pound the shoe into shape and made too much noise to hear anything. When I looked up he was gone. Did he pay you for the work you did today?"

Abe pulled the Spanish bit from his pocket. "Yes, sir. He gave me this. And he wants me to come back on Wednesday to do some more of his records. I guess he doesn't like doing book work, 'cause he seemed real glad that I could do it the way he wanted it."

"Glad to hear that, Abe." As he walked toward the door, Mr. Carson touched the boy's shoulder as he reached for his coat and hat. "Now come on outside while there is still a little daylight and let's get some more firewood ready. May be a hard winter ahead. Everything has seemed a bit strange this year, weatherwise, and there's no telling what winter will bring."

Abe put on his coat, knitted cap and his oldest mittens, and with Towser at his heels, followed his father to the edge of the woods behind the log house where some cut tree trunks lay. When he and his father had one of them placed on the X-shaped "saw horses," each of them grasped an end of the four-foot long crosscut saw Mr. Carson had brought with him, and began to cut the log into short lengths for burning in the cabin fireplace. When they finished cutting that log and were bringing another into position for sawing, Abe decided it was time to find out what his father would say if he got the offer to go to New Orleans on the *Rosalie*.

"Pa, if the captain asks you if I could work on the boat when it leaves to go back to New Orleans, what would you say?"

Mr. Carson carefully lowered his end of the log into position. He straightened up and looked at Abraham. As he struggled to raise his end onto the sawhorse, Abe began to wonder if his father was going to answer at all. When Mr. Carson finally spoke, Abe still did not get his answer.

"There are things to think about, son. For one thing, I count on you to keep the woodbox filled for your mother."

Abe looked at the wood already cut and stacked. The pile had grown each day as he split more logs than were used for cooking and heat in a day's time. "Pa, I'll split and stack wood enough to last, and Hannah can bring it into the house as Mama needs it."

The sun had already gone down and Mr. Carson said, "Let's get this big one cut while we can still see. We'll talk when we go inside." The crosscut saw began to bite into the huge log, a tree trunk three feet in diameter, cut from the woods just beyond the Carson home yard. There was no more talk until the sections, about two feet long, lay on the ground, ready for Abe to split and add to the stack.

"Go to bed, Towser," Abe said and patted the dog on his head. Towser trotted off toward the shed.

It was so dark now that the two could scarcely see their way to the house when the last cut was completed. Mr. Carson took the long saw inside with him to sharpen the jagged teeth.

The girls and their mother had the table cleared and the dishes washed. It was time for the family to gather near the hearth and its blazing fire. Hannah was adding another log as Abe and Mr. Carson took off their coats.

"Beginning to feel like winter might be here," Mr. Carson said. He took his sharpening files from a shelf. "Sit down there, Abe, and hold the saw firmly."

Everyone worked as the next minutes passed. Rachel and Hannah were at the wooden slab table shelling pecans. Mrs. Carson had her knitting needles clicking as she worked the gray yarn she had spun during the summer months into a new stocking cap to keep Abe's head warm for the cold weather.

When each saw tooth had been honed, Mr. Carson said, "Now, then, Abraham, I think your mother would like to know what you have in mind."

Abe placed the newly sharpened saw against the wall beside the outside door. His heart beat faster as he sat down. He swallowed as he thought how to tell his family about his hoped-for job. When he spoke, his voice cracked and squeaked in that annoying way it had begun to do this past year. He hated that, especially when Hannah laughed.

He began. "As I was telling you before, I might get work on a keelboat that is going down to New Orleans. I've been doing some book work for the captain."

Mrs. Carson's knitting needles paused their clicking only for a moment. Then she asked in a quiet voice, "When would the boat be leaving?"

"In a few days, Mama." Silence. He went on, "It's a nice boat, the *Rosalie*. It's nice enough for passengers to travel on it." Abe stopped. Silence again except for the clicking knitting needles and the hammer against nut shells. He shifted in his chair.

"I think I saw the passengers that came up on the *Rosalie*," Hannah said. "They were in Mr. Perry's store—a girl and her father. He called her Antoinette. She was real pretty, but she was having a hard time trying to tell Mr. Perry what she wanted. Guess she doesn't know English very well."

Abe said, "Yes, that was probably them. They'll be goin' back to New Orleans. I heard Captain Byrne telling them they'd leave at the end of this week."

Silence for a moment. Then Mrs. Carson said, "That soon, Abe? I just don't know—"

Mr. Carson spoke up. "I'm not at all sure about the idea, either, Elizabeth. Been a strange year—suffocating hot all summer, and the air was so still. Hot weather all summer often means a bad winter. The river could freeze early, and that means trouble for any boats still traveling."

37

Abe put in, "But, Papa, we'll be goin' south, where it's warmer."

Mrs. Carson said, "That may be, but we know how winter is here. We'll need more wood if it's extra cold—more than is stacked now, Abraham." Abe was about to assure her that he would spend every hour he could cutting and stacking more before he left when she went on. "It was such a strange summer this year. There was rain but no thunderstorms like we always have in spring and summer here. Folks heard sounds like it was thundering down in the ground!"

Hannah said, "I know, Mama. People are still talking about it. I heard that rumbling down in the earth myself, a couple of times. What does it mean, Papa?"

"None of us can answer that one, Hannah. But I am concerned about what might be coming. A lot of people think that comet that we could see most nights was a bad sign, too."

Rachel had stopped cracking nuts to listen. She said, "And in September one day when I was in the store, I heard some boatmen from the Ohio River talking about thousands —maybe millions, they said—of squirrels all running away to the south, like a demon was after them! And lots of them drowned, they said, trying to swim across the Ohio..."

"Now that could be a wild tale, Rachel!" Mr. Carson said. "But I do remember thinking the sun was kind of veiled and strange looking during July and August. And it sure was hot!"

"Well, it worries me," Mrs. Carson said. "If Abe were out on the river and something happened to him, we wouldn't even know for months and months! And besides, I thought river boatmen had to be big, rough fellows."

"That's the crew, Mama," Abe said. "I think I would be doing book work for the captain, cleaning up the passengers' cabins, helping with food—stuff like that."

"Well, Abraham," Mr. Carson said, "as I understand it, you haven't really been offered the job as yet. Is that right?"

Abe was a bit downcast as he answered, "Yes, sir."

"Then let's put off the final decision until he either offers you the job or leaves for New Orleans without you."

Mrs. Carson was tying off the last stitches of the new stocking cap. "This warm cap will be ready for you if you go, Abraham. But I'll have to admit, I'd rather see you wearing it here in St. Louis!"

CHAPTER 4

A Reward for Work Well Done

All day Tuesday, Abe spent every minute that he could splitting and stacking wood. He paused now and then to read again the three lines Colonel Easton had him copy, and before noon he was repeating them from memory as he worked.

At day's end he was the first one to head for bed, a thin straw-stuffed mattress in the loft. "This above all, to thine own self be true—" he said aloud, but a yawn stopped him from going farther. His eyes closed and he was sound asleep.

On Wednesday morning before breakfast, he and his father put in an hour sawing up large limbs from the tree on which they had worked on Monday evening. After breakfast, Abe washed his hands and face, combed his hair, put on a better shirt, and headed toward the riverfront.

He was passing the post office when Colonel Easton hailed him. "Abraham, are you going down to the landing?"

"Yes, sir. Captain Byrne has some work for me to do on the *Rosalie.*"

"Please tell him that the mail came over on the ferry from Illinois, bringing more packets and packages for him to take downriver, and not to leave without them."

"I'll tell him for sure, Colonel. Did he tell you when he's heading downriver?"

"He thought he'd be embarking at dawn Saturday, Abe. Any chance of your being on board then?"

"I still haven't been offered a job. But I think I'll find out today for sure. If you see my father, tell him again you think it would be good for me to go—please?"

"Sure will, Abe. In fact, I have a little extra time right now, and I'll walk over to his shop and talk with him. As I see it, working on a boat for that long voyage will help you grow up. You might even have a good idea of what you want to work at the rest of your life." Colonel Easton paused, but continued to gaze intently at Abe. "Learned those lines by heart yet?"

Abe grinned. "Sure have. I think I can even say them in my sleep. Thanks, Colonel Easton," he said, and went on his way.

He hadn't gone a block farther when he saw Gus Perkins at the next cross street, heading downhill toward the river. Gus stopped when he saw Abe coming toward him.

"Thought you were pretty smart the other day, didn't you?" he called as Abe drew near. "You sure did your best to get me in bad with that boat captain."

"Somebody had to stop that guy from getting on the boat. Don't blame me 'cause you fell asleep on the job."

"All you needed to do was holler to me and I'd have seen him comin'. But no, you had to be a smarty and dump him in the river yourself. Well, let me tell you, Abraham Carson, I can knock you down like you was nothin', you sawed off runt."

41

"Yeah. I s'pose you could. Your arms are long enough, but you're kind of short, too. Short on good sense."

Gus stood still, fists clenched, red-faced with anger. He seemed stunned at what Abe had dared to say. Abe decided maybe he'd made a mistake and was about to be beaten up. He used the moment to start running toward the riverfront.

Gus was right behind him before he had gone a block, moving fast for once. "Got enough sense to beat you up, smart-aleck Abe," Gus snarled, and Abe felt his coat collar grabbed at the back. He lost his balance and a second later was lying on his back in the dirt street, with Gus straddling him.

"You fixed it so's I couldn't get that job going downriver on that boat, you little sneak," Gus was saying. "I'd have had that cabin boy job if you hadn't stuck your nose into my business!"

Abe was struggling to get to his feet, but Gus hovered over him, with his fists clenched. *If I get up, he'll beat up on me,* Abe thought. He'd try an old trick.

"So maybe the captain figured you'd sleep all the way down the river," he said. Then, suddenly, he cried out and pointed down toward the river. "Look! Here he comes now!"

Gus half turned to see if Abe was telling the truth, and Abe quickly took hold of his attacker's left leg and pulled. As Gus lost his balance and fell, Abe escaped and ran on down the street. But Gus was only a few steps behind him before he had gone another block.

Captain Byrne was indeed out on the street, but not walking toward the boys. He was a block away, where the street ended and the levee began, deep in conversation with the gentleman who had come upriver on the *Rosalie*. Antoinette was standing beside her father. Abe slowed down to a walk, sure that Gus wouldn't dare knock him down again where there would be witnesses.

He heard Gus, right behind him, muttering, "You tricked me! Boy, I'll get you for sure when you can't hide behind a girl's skirts!"

Antoinette turned to watch the two boys approaching. Looking at Abe, she said, "'Allo, nice boy! I learn English now." The words sounded a little strange, but Abe understood them.

Grinning, he said, "You're doing great, Miss Antoinette."

Gus walked by the two of them and stood so close to the captain that both men stopped talking. Captain Byrne said, "Yes, what do you want?"

"I'm your new cabin boy, Captain. One of your men said you would be needing a boy to go down to New Orleans."

"You heard wrong. I've already found a cabin boy. Now get out of here and don't pester me again. If I did need a boy, you'd be the last one I'd consider."

All Gus could do was stammer, "Uh—I thought maybe—" but the captain had turned away from him. Gus glared at Abe as he turned and walked away.

Abe was near enough to have heard the captain's words. He had a sinking feeling in his stomach. The job was

43

already filled. There would be no trip to New Orleans for him. But Antoinette was smiling at him and he tried to smile back.

Captain Byrne had seen Abe. His voice was a little less gruff as he said, "Go on board, Abraham. I'll be in to show you the book work in just a few minutes."

Abe smiled at Antoinette and pulled at his stocking cap as if he were tipping his hat in gentlemanly style, and then walked on along the levee to the *Rosalie* and up the gangplank. A bit dejected, he pulled back the curtain and entered the captain's cabin.

For a moment, as he stood just inside the curtain, he noticed that the captain had hung his working clothing on wall pegs to the left of the door. His extra boots were beneath them. He seemed to be neat in his habits. *Sure wish I was going to work for him longer*—he thought. His eyes went to the cupboard in the back corner. For a moment, he considered peaking inside it to see what was on that mysterious paper that seemed to upset the captain so.

To thine own self be true—Abe was startled at how clearly he heard Colonel Easton's words. "No," he said aloud, and turned away. On the desk, the record book was open to a page with only a heading on it—*"Rosalie,* embarking December 7, 1811. Bill of Lading."

That's Saturday, Abe thought, *and I won't be going.* For some reason, he thought then of Antoinette and her smiling dark eyes as she had looked only a few minutes ago. *Guess I'll never see her again.*

He sighed, and turned back to the book. Loose papers with notes written on them were scattered about on the table. As he waited, Abe wondered who had been chosen to be cabin boy on the Rosalie. Likely one of the boys he'd gone to school with. His mind was still checking off the likely candidates when he heard the heavy steps of Captain Byrne, and the curtain to the cabin was pushed aside.

"I want you to write the cargo list for this voyage, Abe. That's what the 'Bill of Lading' means. Each of these loose pages has information that's to go on this page. I'll do one to show you how to do it."

As the captain touched the pen point to the book page, a drop of ink fell from it, and he swore as he reached for the blotting paper.

"See why I want someone to do my book work?" he asked Abe as he soaked up the ink with the blotting paper.

Abe smiled as he thought, *Just like me! Even the captain makes blots.* After the captain had demonstrated how to transfer the information from the papers to the page in the book, he left the cabin. "I'll be away from the *Rosalie* for about an hour, Abraham, and I'll look for you here when I get back. If you need anything, Barney is here and you can ask him."

Abe sighed as he turned his mind to the work before him. Later, he'd ask Barney who got the cabin boy job. Looking at the papers, he noticed that most of the shipments were of furs, some of the pelts that the voyageurs had brought down the Missouri River. Listed were bundles of beaver pelts, of "bear skins, black, gray, yellow and brown," of deer skins "in the hair," and "dressed," of "bison hides or robes," and smaller amounts of fox, otter, and raccoon skins.

As Abe copied the information, his mind wandered to the wilderness he imagined but had never seen. Maybe he'd like to be a fur trader, like the ones who had brought all these furs to St. Louis.... He turned back to the few papers left to be entered, some barrels of salt from "Boone's Lick" up the Missouri River about a hundred miles, some barrels of hemp rope, a few of wine, and a shipment of "bear's grease" from the same area.

He was entering the last bill of lading into the record book when Captain Byrne returned.

"Through already with that stack?" The captain seemed surprised as Abe added the last one to the stack. But he only grunted and began leafing through the pages, checking to see if the information was correctly written in the book. When he had finished he grunted again. Abe took the grunt to mean he had done the work well.

"Should I go now?" he asked when Captain Byrne seemed satisfied. He hoped there would be some more work he could do, to earn a bit more before the *Rosalie* departed.

"Not yet, Abe. I'd like to show you where you'll bunk."

Abe was startled. "What do you mean, sir?"

"You heard me tell that loafer that I had found a cabin boy, didn't you?"

"Yes, sir. But you didn't say who he was."

46

"Well, the job is yours if you want it. While I was in town I talked to your father and got his permission for you to ship out with us."

Abe's mouth hung open. "You d-did? I mean, he did?"

"Had to explain to him that I wouldn't put you on the regular crew, handling the oars and poles, and you'd have a bunk near me and Barney."

Abe's heart was going so fast and hard he thought the captain might even hear it. He took a deep breath to calm himself and then asked, "What work will I be doing, sir?"

"I'll expect you to be ready to help handle the lines when we are docking or embarking, to do more of this kind of paper work to keep track of shipments and deliveries, to clean the passengers' cabins and other parts of the boat, and help the cook. Think you can handle that?"

Abe nodded his head and gulped. His voice squeaked as he said, "I'd sure like to try, Captain."

"Barney took a liking to you the day you dumped that fellow into the river. Look to him for answers to questions you have. Agreed?"

"Y-yes, sir,"

"Then shake hands on it." The captain's hand shake was the firmest Abe had ever experienced. His hand hurt a bit from the captain's grip, but the grin on his face didn't change.

"Now come over here and I'll show you where you'll bunk. Then you can get on home. Your father says you'll need to split some more wood before we leave here early on Saturday. I'll want you on board by three in the afternoon Friday. That's day after tomorrow. Think you can make it?"

☒ ☒ ☒

The rest of the day Abraham's mind was far from the work he was doing to build up the wood pile. When he came in for supper, his mother looked at him with a worried expression.

"Abraham, are you sure you want to go on that boat?"

"Yes, Mama. I know I can do the work—except maybe the part about helping the cook. I'm not very good at that. Hannah and Rachel do that part around here."

"I'm sure you can peel potatoes and that kind of work the cook will need you for. What I'm worried about is what might happen on the way down to New Orleans."

"Like what, Mama?"

"Like the boat being wrecked by a snag and sinking. Like river pirates attacking and robbing—or even killing you. And the weather has been so strange—what if a terrible storm came up and you lost—"

"Oh, Mama! Those things won't happen. Captain Byrne knows the river well and how to keep out of trouble."

"I surely hope so. But even he can't control the weather, and there could be bad storms—" Mrs. Carson was frowning. "And how will we know that you are safe?"

"You'll just have to know that, Mama, and not be worrying all the time. I'm almost a man now." His voice chose that moment to crack and squeak. He cleared his throat and went on. "Mama, I've got to begin taking care

48

of myself. Please don't worry! I'll send a letter as soon as I can. Maybe we'll meet a boat coming upriver and someone can tell you I'm fine."

Mrs. Carson patted his shoulder. "I'll try not to worry, Abe. But you'll be gone a long time. The keelboat won't be coming back up the river until the winter ends. I'm just glad that your Uncle Daniel and Aunt Mattie are in New Orleans, and I want you to promise you'll go to their house as soon as Captain Byrne lets you leave the boat."

"I will, Mama. Just tell me how to find their house and I'll stay with them if they'll let me."

"They'll let you, I'm sure. I'll write a letter for you to take along, and you can give it to them right away. But I do want you to find things to do around their house to help pay for your keep."

"Yes, Mama. I'll do everything they want me to. And Captain Byrne might even have work for me on the river down there where it isn't frozen. I'll be fine—and I will come back home as soon as a boat is coming this way—maybe even with Captain Byrne."

Mrs. Carson kept looking at Abe all through supper, as if she wanted to be sure to remember how he looked. Later she began to get his clothes ready for the long trip, mending rips and patching over a hole in his dungarees, tightening buttons, darning holes in his extra socks.

"You'll need to buy a new pair of boots when you're down in New Orleans, son," she said. "Your feet are growing faster than the rest of you. I'll have this pair of socks finished before you leave, and I'm making them a bit longer than your old ones."

Abe laughed. "If my feet are growing, maybe the rest of me will grow, too, to catch up with them. But Mama, you're working too hard to get my clothes ready. As long as they're clean, that's all that matters."

"And have my brother Daniel and his wife see you with holes in your socks and rips in your pants? No, sir. I'm going to send you looking fine." She went on with the knitting. After a moment, she sighed. "It may be a long time before you can get back—and I'll feel better about you if I send you away with at least one extra pair of socks." Then she let her knitting needles stop their constant clicking and looked over at Abe.

"Son, I can't help worrying about you going so far from home—and with winter setting in, it will be such a long time before there'll be a boat to bring you back. And I have this strange feeling—" her voice was suddenly tight, and when Abe looked up there were tears in her eyes.

"Mama, don't feel bad. The *Rosalie* is a good boat, and Captain Byrne has taken her up and down the Mississippi several times. He knows how to watch out for snags and river pirates, and he'll be careful." Noticing how alarmed his mother looked at the mention of the real dangers on the river, Abe smiled and added, "Besides, he's got cargo too valuable to take chances. He doesn't want to lose the money from all those furs we're takin' downriver! He'll be mighty careful, on account of them. So I'll be safe, along with the furs."

Mrs. Carson smiled faintly. Then she said, "I can't help but worry. I have this awful feeling of something bad about to happen—maybe because it's been such a strange year."

Mr. Carson looked up from the newspaper he was reading. "We mustn't spend the time worrying about him, Elizabeth," he said. "It will really be a good experience for Abraham, I think. Teach him a lot about the world out there."

Abe thought, *I can tell that Papa listened to Colonel Easton. He's sure a nice man.*

His father continued speaking, "I met the two passengers who will also be on the boat, a very fine French gentleman and his daughter. The girl is about Hannah's age. Captain Byrne brought them along when he came to talk to me this morning. He said he needed a boy on this trip mostly to take care of the passengers. His crew can handle the boat, but none of the men would have time to clean the cabins and do other things the girl and her father might need."

Abe turned to his father, a wide smile on his face. "She's pretty, isn't she, Papa?"

Mr. Carson looked sharply at his son. "So you noticed that, did you? Yes, she's pretty, but girls aren't what I meant that you'd learn about, son."

Hannah and Rachel were struggling with the knitting they were learning to do, making wool scarves. Both had been listening to the conversation, and Hannah said, "If that French girl's going, maybe I'd better go along, too! I could clean the passenger's cabins better than Abe. He wouldn't even think about whether the girl needed a clean towel or things like that."

"Don't even joke about your leaving, too, Hannah!" Mrs. Carson said. "I can't send my two oldest away at the same time."

"No," Mr. Carson said. "Some young man will be taking Hannah away soon enough." At this, Hannah and Rachel looked at each other and burst into giggles.

"Get to bed, you young'uns. Tomorrow's going to be a busy day. You, too, Abe. We've got a lot of wood still to be split and stacked!"

CHAPTER 5

All Aboard to a New World

"May I come aboard, Captain Byrne?"

It was three o'clock on Friday, December 6, a bright sunny day but with a chill in the air. Abe stood at the foot of the gangplank, carrying his blanket roll with his clothing packed inside it. He had worked since dawn, cutting and stacking so much firewood that he was sure his family would have some left when he returned. And all the time his mind had been on this moment and the adventure to come.

Captain Byrne's gruff voice called out, "Abe, thought you'd changed your mind. Stow your gear under Barney's bunk."

Abe noticed that the *Rosalie* looked quite different now that it was almost time to start down the river. As he had approached her, he caught a glimpse of the aft deck, now almost at water level for the weight of the filled barrels stored there. On the cabin roof, the sail was roped to the mast, ready for use when the weather was right. The "cordelle" was neatly coiled on the forward deck, near the prow. Most of the crew would sleep on that deck wherever there was space. When the *Rosalie* was not at a stop along the way, the food would be cooked there on an iron grate set up in a sheet metal sand box where the fire could be built. The crew's blanket rolls were nearby, covered by pieces of sail cloth to serve as tenting in case of rain. Daytimes, the deck was left open alongside the gunwales, except for crude bench seats where the men would sit when it was time to man the oars. They were seldom needed on the downriver voyage.

An open area led from the end of the gangplank to the low cabin doorway where the captain awaited Abe, who followed him down the two steps.

"Here's Barney's bunk, and yours is above it." Captain Byrne indicated an area across from his cabin with two narrow wooden bunks, each with a thin mattress. "Sometimes Barney snores a mighty roar," he added. "If he wakes you, just reach down and wake him up. He's real obligin' about turnin' over."

Abe had not heard the captain laugh before, as he did now. He began to wonder if there was some joke behind his statement about Barney's being "real obligin'" when awakened in the night. The captain's face wore his usual serious expression when he continued speaking. "Get your gear stowed, Abe. I've got an errand for you."

Abe was to go up to the post office to get the mail that was to be taken to the few small settlements southward along the river or on to New Orleans. "Before you go, ask Barney if there are any other errands."

Abe walked toward the stern on the cleated "running board," in the narrow space, about eighteen inches wide alongside the cabin. When the river was not too deep for the twenty foot setting poles to reach the river bottom, the men worked there, using the poles to propel the boat. The cleats were to help the men get a firm footing. It was known as the "running board" because to help the boat move, the men ran a few feet to get the full effect of the long poles' push.

At the back of the cabin, Barney was directing the stowing of packs of pelts being hoisted on board by crewmen. He looked up when he heard Abe's call. "Hallo, there, Matey Abe!" he called out. "Nearly ready for your first night's sleep on board the *Rosalie?*"

For the first time, the hours ahead became real to Abe. He envisioned the narrow plank where he would be perched for the night. *What if I fall out in my sleep?* His grin was a bit sickly as he answered Barney. "I guess so. Cap'n said I should ask you if there was anythin' else you need in town. I'm goin' up to the post office."

"You could stop at the carpenter's shop on your way back, Abe," Barney said. "James has been shapin' up a new rudder end for the steerin' pole. The old one was gettin' kind of rotten. James didn't have it quite finished when I stopped there this mornin', but he was gettin' right onto it. Find out if it's ready."

"Sure thing," Abe said.

Barney called out, as Abe walked back to the gangplank, "And ask him if he's got another left-hand hammer."

"Yes, sir, Mr. Barney."

Barney was grinning when Abe looked back, but he quickly changed to a serious expression. "You can forget the mister, Matey. Just plain Barney."

It didn't take long for Abe to reach Colonel Easton's house. No one was in the little post office, so he rang the bell. The postmaster himself called out, "Be there in a minute. Hold your horses while I finish this line."

"It's just me, Colonel—Abe Carson. I've come to get the rest of the stuff for the *Rosalie.*"

About five minutes later, Easton appeared in the doorway, in his shirt sleeves and wearing an eyeshade. "Had to finish copying that affidavit. Now if I had a smart young fellow like you studying law with me, I could have him taking care of such clerk's work." He looked meaningfully at Abe, shook his head sadly, and said, "Guess you're still bound and determined to be a boatman instead of a lawyer."

"I think I might get to be a boat captain, like Captain Byrne."

"Hmmph. Don't get to be a captain until you can buy your own keelboat. Costs a lot of money, Abraham, and you'd have to save all you earned doing the hard boatman's work first."

"But I'd be going places, like to New Orleans."

The postmaster was bringing a bulging canvas sack from the back of the room. He set it in front of Abe, and as he straightened up he pushed back his eyeshade, put his hands on his hips and gazed at Abe.

"You think lawyers don't go places, Abe? Sometimes we go a long way to fight a case or an appeal—like to Washington, to the Supreme Court. I expect I'll go to Washington myself before many years go by. More and more people have been coming to this territory, and it needs a man in Congress to speak for the people. I'm likely to

56

be that man, Abraham. I intend to run for office, and usually a lawyer gets elected."

Abe was surprised at this news. "Gee, Washington is even farther away than New Orleans! Would your clerk go with you?"

"Sure enough, lad. But we'd better get you on the way now with this mail sack. Put it over your shoulder to carry it. And *bon voyage!* Come in when you get back."

"Yes, sir. And thanks for talking to my father." Abe hefted the clumsy sack over his left shoulder and held it by the cords that closed it. "So long, Colonel!"

"So long, Abraham! Remember that advice from old Shakespeare, 'To thine own self be true.'"

As he started down the road, Abe called back, "Yes, sir! I won't forget!" Then he stopped for a moment and turned around. The lawyer was standing outside, smoking his cigar. Abe called out, "And it must follow, as the night the day—I can't then be false to any man!" The last Abe saw of Colonel Easton, the lawyer was waving his cigar on the air in a cheery goodbye.

Abe walked on toward the carpenter's shop. By the time he reached it, the sack was feeling twice as heavy. He set it down beside the shop entrance, and looked up just in time to see Gus Perkins' lanky figure entering the shop from the rear. Gus was carrying a length of rough cut lumber. He put the wood down on the dirt floor and saw Abe as he straightened up. His expression changed to a sneer.

"Well, look who's here. The sneaky kid that took my job on the keelboat. Think I can't get a job, don'tcha? Well, I got me a boat job anyway."

The carpenter came in from a side room at that moment and Abe decided it was best to ignore Gus.

"Barney, from Captain Byrne's keelboat, asked me to see if the rudder was ready, Mr. James."

"You bet it is. James always keeps his word. Just a minute until I take care of this delivery." He examined the wood Gus had brought. "Not too good, Gus, but it will do. Tell your father I'll pay him next week." He turned back to Abe. "Now then, we'll get the rudder."

Abe remembered his other errand. "Oh—Mr. James, Barney said I should see if you have a left-hand hammer for him." He heard a guffaw from Gus, who had not left the shop.

Mr. James, hands on his hips, leaned back and laughed. "Think about it, Abe. What would a left-hand hammer look like?"

Abe looked puzzled. Then he grinned. "Same as a right-hand one! Ain't no such thing, is there, Mr. James?"

"Right, lad. Barney was funnin' you. Tell him we'uns was all out of them hammers, but we've got some good sky hooks."

He laughed as he said that, and Abe laughed, too. "I'll sure tell him, Mr. James. And that you'll have a left-hand hammer for him next trip."

James went to the next room and as he brought back the rudder, he said, "This is heavy, lad. Think you can carry it?"

Gus had made no move to leave and stood watching as Abe picked up the rudder, a plank about three feet long, eighteen inches wide, and two inches thick. "It is kind of heavy, Mr. James. I'll take the mail sack down to the *Rosalie* and then come right back for it." He leaned the rudder against the wall.

Gus strode over to the rudder. "Out of the way, little boy. Let a man handle that rudder. Huh! I could carry that with one hand and the mail sack with the other! The captain shouldn't have hired a runt like you."

"Let's see you carry it with one hand, if you're so smart, Gus. I dare you to take it all the way to the *Rosalie* without usin' two hands. Betcha a bit you can't do it!"

Gus sneered. "I'm gonna take that bet, you little shrimp. Let's see if you've got a bit to pay off with."

Abe pulled one from his trouser pocket. "Now let's see yours, Gus."

From inside his shirt, Gus drew a small leather sack hung by a thong around his neck. "It's in here. Now let's get goin'."

Abe took the canvas sack as Gus picked up the board, and with some difficulty, balanced and braced it against his side so that he could carry it with his right hand.

"Go ahead, Gus. Remember, you lose if you touch the rudder with your left hand after we start. I'll be right behind you to make sure you don't cheat," Abe said.

There were only two blocks to go to the riverfront where the *Rosalie* was tied. Gus ambled along carrying the rudder board without too much difficulty. Abe began to think he'd lose the bet, but at least the board would be delivered and there wasn't much time left before dark. *It's worth a bit to get it delivered*, he thought.

They reached the sloping levee. Ahead, near the *Rosalie's* gangplank, they saw two of the crew members carrying the trunk and carpet bags that belonged to the passengers. Antoinette and her father followed close behind. Barney and Captain Byrne were on the deck to welcome them aboard.

Gus was about twenty feet ahead of Abe and starting down the slope when Antoinette turned and saw the two boys coming. She waved, recognizing Abe, and came toward them. Gus saw this as a gesture toward himself and raised his left arm to wave. The rudder tilted forward and he had to grasp it quickly with both hands to keep it from falling.

As Abe waved to Antoinette, he saw Gus's sudden movement. "Aha! You're using both hands, Gus!" he yelled. "You lose the bet!"

At this, Gus decided to drop the rudder. It fell to the sandy levee soil without damage to it, but its fall was broken by a corner striking Gus's boot toe. "Ow!" he cried. And then he swore loudly.

Antoinette was quite close to the boys. "Oh! What he say?" she cried. "Big boy very—how you say it, *en colère!*"

"Hello, Miss Antoinette!" Abe called. "I think you mean angry. Don't mind Gus. He's kind of mad at me."

Abe had caught up with Gus. "Hey, Gus, thanks for bringin' the rudder for me. You lost the bet, but you don't owe me that bit 'cause you brought the board nearly to the boat. Fair trade."

"Yeah. Thanks for nothin'," Gus muttered. He was keeping his voice down, but as he turned to look at Abe there was hatred in his eyes. He made no attempt to pick up the rudder from where it lay on the ground.

Barney came hurrying up. "Miss Antoinette, your father says for you to come back to the boat, please." Then he turned to Abe. "I didn't mean for you to try to bring back that rudder, Abe. I just meant for you to find out if it was ready, and I'd send one of the men for it."

He paused before picking the rudder up, looking down at Gus, who had sat down and pulled off his boot. He was rubbing his toes through a big hole in his sock. "Well, thanks, Gus. Nice of you to carry the rudder and save us the trouble. Sorry you hurt your toes. Should have been using both hands to carry this heavy thing. Here's something for your trouble." Barney had pulled out his money sack and was holding out a bit.

Gus pulled his boot back on and stood up. "Don't want your old money. Don't need no job, neither. Got one on a better boat than your old *Rosalie.*" He started to walk away, but first he turned to Abe, scowling. "I'll get you for this. Just you wait and see."

"Yeah. See you down the river," Abe said. He was sure that Gus was lying about having a job on a better boat. There just wasn't any boat at the St. Louis landing that was even half as nice as the *Rosalie.* A small keelboat that was going to take on a load of lead down at Saint Genevieve had been docked near the Rosalie but had left

61

the day before. A large flatboat was being loaded farther up the levee. Abe couldn't see how any flatboat could compare with the *Rosalie*. That must be the boat that Gus was going on.

As Abe went on board with the mail sack, he said, "Barney, Mr. James is makin' you a left-hand hammer for next time you're in port."

Barney's eyes had a gleam as he looked back at Abe.

Abe added, "And he said he had a fine sky hook for you. Should I go back and get it?" They both had a good laugh as Barney stowed the mail sack just inside the captain's cabin.

⌛ ⌛ ⌛

The next hour went quickly. Abe was kept very busy seeing that the passengers were brought everything they needed. Since they had come from New Orleans on this same keelboat, they were not in need of much help. They knew more about the boat than Abraham did.

When everything seemed to be done, Abe told the captain he was going home for supper, as had been arranged, and would be back soon afterward. He was to spend the night on board because the *Rosalie* would be starting down the river at the first light of dawn. This would be his last meal with his family for a long time.

As he stepped out of the cabin, Antoinette was standing on the deck, looking over toward the Illinois shore. She turned as she heard Abe calling goodbye to Captain Byrne and said, "Abraham, I talk to you, please?" Abe stopped and she came close to him.

"Hello, Miss Antoinette," he said. "I am glad you're gonna be on the boat, too." He smiled, suddenly bashful as those lively dark brown eyes looked into his. He felt himself blushing and he hoped she didn't notice.

"*Mon père*—Papa—say you help me learn English, *peut-être*, yes?" Her voice lifted as she asked the question, gazing into Abe's eyes.

Abe stammered, "Uh—I'd like to, if the captain will let me, Miss Antoinette." His voice squeaked on the girl's name.

"You can call me Toni, Abraham. No 'miss.'"

Abe liked the way she said Abraham. He swallowed hard and said, "You can call me Abe, Toni." They stood looking at each other for a moment and then Abe said, "I gotta go, Toni." Suddenly conscious that he might be teaching her poorly, he said, "I mean, I must leave now. I am going to my home for supper, but I will be back later." He smiled and waved as he left the boat.

It was nearly mid-December and darkness came fast.

His mother had prepared his favorite meal—her stewed chicken and dumplings with creamy gravy. After dessert of apple brown betty it was time for him to go back to the *Rosalie*.

As she had promised, his mother had a letter for him to take to Uncle Daniel and Aunt Mattie. When she handed it to him, he could see she was worried. He took the folded paper and put it inside his shirt for safe keeping. He tried not to let her see the tears that were forming in his eyes. He couldn't look at her directly and fussed with buttoning his shirt again until he had control.

63

Then he said, "Mama, I hope you didn't tell Aunt Mattie she should make sure I got plenty of sleep or even that I should be sure to clean my teeth!" He took a deep breath and in his deepest voice said, "After all, Mother, I'm able to take care of myself. I'm fourteen years old!" His voice suddenly squeaked and he cleared his throat quickly.

Mrs. Carson brushed a tear from her cheek before she said, "Never mind what I told your aunt, Abraham. You just remember to behave as your father and I have taught you." She smiled, and the tears came as she added, with a bit of a laugh, "And don't forget to change your socks!" The girls and Abe laughed then, as she wiped her eyes on her apron.

After a moment she regained her composure and added, "And Abraham, please, please send word back to us as soon as you get a chance. Maybe along the way someone will be coming back to St. Louis and will bring a message that you are all right. And I'll want to know you have arrived at New Orleans safely. I'll worry until I hear that you are all right. Especially when I know such awful things can happen out on that big river. It frightens me."

As his mother talked, Abe felt his own tears pushing their way out again. He gave her a quick kiss and turned his back so that she and the girls would not see that he was crying. He picked up his blanket roll and headed for the door.

Mr. Carson walked out to the street with him. "Son, I've been wanting to tell you that I am proud of you. Can't say such things easily." His voice sounded tight. He held out his big right hand and shook Abe's firmly.

"Goodbye, Pop," was all that Abe could say. He turned and walked rapidly away in the darkness of that December night. It would be a new world that he would be seeing soon, and more adventure than he bargained for.

CHAPTER 6

Abe: Sailor, Teacher and Student

Abe made his way carefully along the dark streets. When he reached the levee he was glad to see a lighted lantern hanging above the cabin doorway of the *Rosalie*. All was quiet, but a dim light also glowed from inside the cabin.

He hurried down the slope to go on board, and discovered the gangplank had been drawn in. Crew members were stretched out, rolled in their blankets and snoring—except for Barney, who was standing, leaning against the cabin door frame. He immediately pushed the gangplank out for Abe.

"Welcome on board, Matey," he said quietly. "Been watchin' fer ya."

As soon as Abe stepped onto the deck, Barney pulled in the plank. "Are the passengers on board already?" Abe whispered.

"Yup. All hands and the passengers are settled for the night. We'll be on our way at dawn, so get yourself in there, lad."

Abe had a sinking feeling in his stomach as he realized that now there was no turning back. It could be spring-time again before he would be back in St. Louis! As he went through the doorway, he shivered, chilled by more than the cold of the night. Inside, he saw that a curtain was drawn across the narrow aisle beyond the captain's quarters and the bunks where he and Barney would be sleeping. Beyond it, Mr. Lagrande and Antoinette would be settling down in their compartments. The light of a candle shone dimly through the curtain. A candle was also still lighted on the captain's table to Abe's right.

Captain Byrne wore a long-sleeved undershirt above his trousers. He pulled back his curtain far enough to see Abe. "It'll seem real strange tonight, lad, but get some sleep if you can," he said in a very low voice. "Never forget my first night on the river. Don't believe I slept a wink." He smiled and looked Abe in the eyes. That hint of a twinkle was there. "You'll do fine, lad. Good night. Don't worry about what time you need to wake up. It's your last chance to sleep in." He disappeared behind the curtain. In a moment, both candles were extinguished.

As Abe climbed up to his bunk, he knew he too would always remember his first night on the river, especially after he bumped his head on the ceiling when he sat up to take off his shirt and boots. Barney, removing his own boots before entering his bunk, whispered, "Next time get all set afore you climb up there, Matey."

Abe's thoughts as he lay in the hard bunk were of home. Had he made a grave mistake? Were his mother's vague premonitions of trouble on the river a sign of what was to come? *No,* he told himself, *it's just the way mothers are. They worry when any of their children leave home. Things will be fine and we'll get to New Orleans in good shape.*

He had almost dropped off to sleep when he heard the first of Barney's snores. *What was it the captain told me?* The words came back, *"Just reach down and wake him up...."*

Abe grasped the side board at the edge of his thin mattress and rolled onto his stomach. He reached down, but couldn't touch Barney. He hung out over the edge as far as he dared without falling, and this time he could reach far enough to touch the snoring man's shoulder. Barney didn't make a move. The snoring just grew into a choking sound followed by a long gargle.

He's real obligin' about wakin' up, the captain had said. So Abe tried again. This time Barney's snore became a snarl and Abe pulled his hand back in alarm. All was quiet for a moment, and he heard a fish splashing hard in the river. *Must have been a really big one! Would have been a great one to catch,* he thought.

Then the snoring resumed, but a bit less intrusive on Abe's thoughts. To keep out the cold air, he rolled up as snugly as he could in his blanket. The water lapped against the boat and he became aware of a gentle rocking motion. Between Barney's loud snores, he listened to all the night sounds—the muffled snores of the men on the deck, the wintry wind that had begun to blow, the creaking of the boat, the coughing of one of the crew, the howl of a coyote from far off.

Suddenly there were two sets of loud snores as Barney's were joined by the sounds from across the aisle where Captain Byrne slept. Abe rolled over, fumbled a bit until he found his new gray stocking cap, and put it on. He pulled it down to cover his ears, and then rolled up tightly in his blankets with his head covered.

The next thing he heard was the sound of someone shouting, "Cast off!" He heard a thump as the gangplank was pulled in for a final time and then the splash of oars in the water as the crew began moving the boat out from the landing.

☒　☒　☒

Dressed in his short dark blue coat over his shirt and trousers, Abe left the deserted cabin and stepped out onto the deck. The *Rosalie* was moving smoothly downriver, surging ahead faster than the current with each stroke of the oars, being pulled by six crewmen seated at the bow of the boat.

"Mornin', Matey!"

It was Barney's hearty voice. Abe looked up and saw his friend on the cabin roof. Behind him the unfurled sail on the mast was belled out with the breeze.

"Mornin', Barney. I didn't even hear you get up."

"I'll be wakin' you after this," Barney said. He waved a hand toward the outdoor galley down on the deck—the sand-filled metal box where a few chunks of charred wood smoldered. "Get some breakfast and then I'll put you to work."

"Yes, sir!" Abe called, but he saw that Barney's attention was no longer on him. It was on the river ahead of the *Rosalie*. His job as mate was to be sure the boat was kept clear of river hazards—sandbars where the *Rosalie* could get stuck for hours, or the hundreds of "snags," the driftwood logs or even whole trees that were in the river.

Abe hastily downed some of the cornbread, bacon and coffee left from the crew's breakfast. The bacon was tough, and the cornbread hard and dry, not like his mother's. The coffee was strong and bitter, but he needed it to wash down the cornbread.

He felt a little tug at his sleeve just as he finished and was putting down the tin cup alongside the firebox.

"Bon matin, nice boy. How you say it in English?"

Abe turned and smiled at Antoinette. *She looks beautiful,* he thought, *in her pretty blue coat and bonnet.* "Good morning—I think that's what you mean, Toni."

"Good mor-ning," she repeated. "Papa—he talk to you."

Mr. Lagrande was behind her. "Yes, young man. Did I hear her call you 'Abe'?"

"Yes, sir. Short for Abraham."

"A very good name, Abraham." Mr. Lagrande spoke English correctly, but with a strong French accent. He said, "I have been trying to teach my daughter to speak English, but I'd like to have her learn it from an American. I thought perhaps you might help her whenever you have some time away from your work. Will you do that?"

Abe was pleased. "Yes, sir. Be glad to, whenever she wants me to and Barney doesn't have work for me." He turned to look quickly at Toni to see if she liked the idea as much as he did. She smiled an answer to his unspoken question.

"C'est bien." Mr. Lagrande absentmindedly spoke in French. Seeing a puzzled look on Abe's face, he said, "Good, very good. You see, Abraham, as soon as I can complete my plans, Toni and I will be returning to St. Louis where I shall be in business. I want her to feel at home with the other young people there."

Abe didn't dare say how pleased he was to hear that, but a broad smile came over his face as he said, "I'll be glad to help her learn American English, sir." He glanced up at Barney and realized he should be starting his work. "See you later, Toni," he said. "I have to get to work now."

As he climbed to the cabin roof, Abe saw that Captain Byrne was back at the stern handling the steering oar. Barney was signaling to the captain that trouble lay ahead. He was pointing to a large mass of tree branches sticking up out of the water alongside an island that they were drawing near on the left.

He called out, "Snag ahead! Pull to the right! Looks like a planter." Then he turned to Abe. "Next to sawyers, them planters are the worst kind of snags. Dang tree's grown roots right into the river bottom." Abe noticed that a moment later the boat swung just slightly toward the shore on the right while still staying in the deeper water.

"Channel's along this side of the island, Abe, but we can't go too close to shore or we'll be in shallow water. You'll get to know this old river and the tricks it can play after you've made a trip or two," Barney said. "But for now, Abe, you'd better get on down and tidy up the cabins."

The Lagrandes, on the deck, had seated themselves on a bench behind the oarsmen, each with a book to read. Abe went inside and pulled aside the curtain leading into their quarters. Mr. Lagrande used one of the four bunks in the men's cabin, just aft of Abe's own. There was another cabin beyond for ladies, where Toni slept in one of the two lower bunks. Abe found the blankets already pulled up neatly on the bunks and clothing hung on the wall pegs. There was little for him to do except to fill the water

71

pitchers with fresh water, dipped from the river, and wipe the wash basins clean.

Then he entered the captain's cabin. Turning to the bunk, he spread the blankets smoothly. There were papers scattered on the table. As he lifted them to put them in better order, he uncovered a sketch done in ink on heavy paper. It was a portrait of a lady. Abe looked at it closely, wondering who she was. *She looks like a real nice lady— pretty, too,* he thought, and placed the sketch carefully under the straightened papers, thinking that Captain Byrne had left it covered, so that was the way he probably wanted it.

After smoothing out his own bunk, Abe folded his extra clothing and put it at the foot end for safekeeping. *One good thing about being short,* he thought, *is there's room left on my bunk to store my things.* His bag and a few extra items were under Barney's bunk, and soon he had that bunk in neat condition too. *Taking care of the cabins will be easy,* he thought.

When Abe returned to the deck he saw that the *Rosalie* was well past the big snag, and had just cleared another island. Now they were rounding a bend in the river. On the roof, Barney was signaling for the boat to move a little farther from shore to miss a large floating log.

Abe went up to get his next orders. Up there, the wind seemed to be trying to push him over. He steadied himself by putting his feet farther apart, and pulled his coat closer around him.

Now I know why sailors walk so funny, he thought. Then he called out against the wind, "What's next, Barney?"

"A bit of a river readin' lesson," Barney said and Abe walked closer to him. "See how different the water looks yonder?" He nodded toward the shore where the water had a brown look, and at the same time he waved his left arm in a signal to the captain. Abe saw the boat's prow point a bit more to the left. "Cap'n's steerin' a bit to port 'cause that's a sandbar yonder. Water's so shallow we could get hung up on it easy as rollin' off a log. Old sandbar's just waitin' there to grab our keel so's we'd all have to jump in the water and lift her to get the *Rosalie* free. If we didn't jump in and get her loose, we'd be sittin' here till the ice came, and then we'd have to wait till it melted next spring!"

Barney laughed, but Abe shivered at the thought of cold winter winds that might come soon. Barney continued to scan the water as they eased past the sandbar.

"What's next for me to do, Barney?"

Glancing down at the deck below, Barney said, "Look's like Mike could use a hand with checkin' the cordelle. Get on down there."

Mike was the crew member who took Barney's place from time to time, next in command. He was uncoiling the long rope known by the French name, "cordelle," checking it for weakened places. The crew had had to "cordelle" over and over again on the way upriver when there had been no way to move the *Rosalie*. This meant the men had to get into the water or onto the river bank to drag her onward until the current weakened enough for poles and oars to move her on.

"Good to have you aboard, Abe," Mike said. "We'll make a river man out of you right soon. Keep layin' this old line in a good coil as I check her."

When Mike found a slightly frayed place, he showed Abe to how to wrap it with oakum, loose fiber that was always carried on a voyage for repair work. Near the oakum, there was a small barrel of tar and an iron spreading tool to make the mending fiber secure.

"Same stuff we use to fill a crack in the hull to keep out the water," Mike explained.

When this task was finished, it was time to help the cook with the noon meal. Afterwards, when the clean-up was done, Abe was free for a time. Mr. Lagrande and Toni were sitting on a bench on the deck.

"If you like, we can work on Toni's English lesson now, Mr. Lagrande," Abe said.

Toni smiled and nodded. Her father said, "Very good, Abe. Tell her all the words you think of as we go along —names of things we see or use, and have her repeat what you tell her."

Abe enjoyed himself immensely as he told Toni the English words for her coat and bonnet, and the color they were. "Blue, like the sky." He pointed up as he said this.

"Coat up there?"

"No, no, Toni." Abe saw that he would have to be more careful in his teaching. He spent the next few minutes in teaching her what coats were, and what was meant by "sky." But when he pointed to the sky the next time, a bank of clouds had moved in and it was no longer blue.

"The sky is not blue," Toni said, very carefully.

"Part of it is now gray," Abe said. "But look back there—what do you see?"

"The sky is blue," Toni said, and smiled happily. "I learn English, Abe! There the sky is *très* bleu. How you say it?"

"There the sky is very blue."

Barney called to Abe to come up to the cabin roof again, and the English lesson came to a quick end. As he walked away, Abe heard Toni practicing. "See the blue sky. The sky is very blue. There the sky is gray. It is not blue. The coat is blue—"

When Abe was beside him, Barney pointed down river. "Now just ahead, Matey, is a place called Herculaneum and we're gonna make a stop there."

"What for, Barney?"

"See that tower on top of that rocky bluff and the little village off to the right? They's lead mines farther in from the river, to the west, and what they do with it is what we're stoppin' to get."

Abe was a bit mystified. "Is the tower so's they can see what's comin' down the river?" he asked.

"Might be they do that, too. But it's called a shot tower. Just put up this year. You'll see what it's for. Now get down to the deck and uncoil the line for the dockin'."

There wasn't much of a landing at Herculaneum, just a narrow strip of grassy land beyond and below the steep-sided rocky bluff on which the tower had been built.

The *Rosalie* was guided beyond the base of the cliff and moved close to a small pier.

When the line was fast, Captain Byrne and three men of the crew left the boat and headed uphill to a small log building at the base of the tower. Abe and Barney stopped to watch the work going on at the tower.

With ropes and pulleys, workmen were hoisting a large bucket to the top, being very careful to avoid tipping it. Two more men stood on a small platform at the tower's top.

"Now, Abe, watch and you'll see that they pour out what's in the bucket, which happens to be lead melted down and still mighty hot. It'll come outta that there spout up on the platform, real slow like. Funny thing, but it cools fast and forms drops that get round as they fall." He bent over and picked up a little round silvery ball from the ground and gave it to Abe.

Abe was surprised. "Why, that's a bit of shot for a gun!"

"Right you are, and that's why they call that a shot tower."

Captain Byrne came from the building following two of the crew. Each of them was carrying a wooden keg which appeared to be very heavy. He said, "Abe, go on board and get a blank bill of lading from the table in my cabin."

Abe was glad to have a job to do. He brought the paper to the captain, who grunted as he took it and then said, "Come with me." Abe followed him into the building.

A man was scooping shot from a bin along the wall nearest to the shot tower and pouring it into a keg. Four

76

more kegs, lids fastened onto them, stood ready for the men from the *Rosalie* to carry out to the boat.

As the man straightened up from his task, Captain Byrne said, "Mr. Matlock, like you to meet Abe Carson, my new clerk." He added to Abe, "Mr. Matlock owns this shot tower."

Abe was startled and delighted to hear himself introduced as the captain's clerk. Mr. Matlock shook his hand, looking almost as startled as Abe to see a boy so young-looking in a responsible job.

"Abe'll write out the bill of lading, Mr. Matlock," the captain said, and nodded for Abe to go over to a high table that served as a desk. "Make it out to Matlock and Company, Herculaneum, Missouri." Then he turned back to Matlock and continued their conversation. "May be a big war between England and the United States starting before long. The militia down in New Orleans wants all the shot and other munitions they can get."

"So I heard, Captain. Matter of fact, that's why I built this tower, near the lead mines and close to the river." Matlock put the lid on the keg of shot. "That makes six, ready to go, Captain."

Abe completed the bill of lading, with a new feeling of pride in work he could do. Then he and Captain Byrne were ready to leave the office. Matlock shook hands with the captain and offered a hand to Abe, saying, "Nice to meet you, Mr. Carson."

Abe was so startled to hear himself addressed as Mr. Carson that he looked up for a moment to see if his father had somehow appeared in the room. Trying to sound quite grown up, he said, "Thank you, Mr. Matlock. Glad to meet you, too." His voice chose to squeak on the last word, and he felt himself blushing.

After he took the bill of lading to the captain's cabin, Paul, the crew member who doubled as cook, called him. He was going to cook the evening meal on shore, and Abe was to start getting wood for the fire. They would eat there and then move on down the river as far as they could before dark.

While Paul and Abe worked on getting a meal ready, Patrick chopped down a small tree and sawed it into short lengths to add to the wood supply for future use. With Paul tending the actual cooking, Abe helped by splitting the firewood chunks. Doing work he had done often at home made him a bit homesick. He was brought back to the present abruptly by the sound of rifle fire from farther in the woods.

"What's that? Who's shooting?" Abe cried.

"Don't worry. No Indians are coming after us! Likely it was Mike bringing down a wild turkey," said Paul. A few minutes later he was proved right. Mike came back carrying a large turkey by the feet.

"Tomorrow's dinner," he said as he began the job of "dressing" his prey.

Toni came ashore to watch the preparations for supper, and when it was ready she and her father joined the crew as they ate sitting on the riverbank. Soon it was time to get on board and underway once more. A strong wind had come up and the sun was setting, although it was hidden by clouds.

"We won't get very much farther before night," the captain said as he mounted the ladder to take the rudder pole. "Keep an eye out for a good place to tie up, Barney."

They had gone only a mile or so when Toni walked up to Abe and tugged at his sleeve. She pointed skyward and said, "The sky is not blue!"

"You remembered our lesson—and you are right," Abe said, looking up and toward the west. "Over there it is almost black!"

Dark clouds were moving in very fast and the wind suddenly became stronger than before.

Barney came down from the cabin roof. "Miss Antoinette," he said. "There's a storm brewin'. You'd best get inside to your cabin. Abe, we're goin' in to a cove just around that bend to ride this out. Get the lines ready. Mike, help me furl the sail." Barney scrambled back up the ladder with Mike at his heels, as the other men worked with oars and poles to guide the boat.

A minute or two later, when Barney and he had the sail closed and tied to the mast, Mike came down from the roof. He pulled a large canvas from a pile on the deck and said, "Here, Abe, help me get the canvas over our gear!" Abe learned in a hurry how to handle the covering that would keep the blanket rolls, food and fuel supplies and cooking gear reasonably dry.

The rest of the crew all worked to move the boat safely around the bend and head it for shelter from the storm. Rain came pouring down before they finally had the *Rosalie* well into the sheltering cove and the lines secured around two stout trees, one at the prow and the other near the stern.

79

The wind swooped down into the cove as if trying its best to push the boat back into open water.

As the men, chilled through and wet, were clambering back on board after securing the lines, the wind howled louder than ever. The boat creaked at each joint, straining against its lines. The line at the prow stretched out so tightly that it seemed it must surely snap in two.

And then, as the hull tipped dangerously, there came a sound like the yowl of a bobcat in pain.

CHAPTER 7

Problems, Progress and Pirates

"We've hit a snag for sure!" Barney yelled. "Cap'n! I'm gonna check it!" He pulled off his boots, climbed over the gunwales and disappeared.

He had hardly landed in the water, no deeper than to his waist, when there was sudden calm. The fierce wind died. Five more crewmen went overboard to help free the *Rosalie* from whatever she had hit, moving her slightly closer to shore as the line at the prow relaxed a little.

"Keep it up!" Barney yelled from his position in the water. "A little more'n' we can free her from this jagged stump she's hung up on. But a board is splintered—we'll need to beach her quick afore more water gets in."

Captain Byrne pulled in the rudder pole and laid it on the roof. He called out orders to his crew. "Mike and Josh, loosen the stern line." When the boat was free, Paul tossed the *cordelle* to the men to tow the Rosalie farther into the cove to get the broken hull board above the water-line. It took a mighty effort, as darkness quickly descended. With the boat slanting a bit downhill, but held firmly by the lines fore and aft to trees on the river bank, the dripping wet men came on board to try to rest for the night.

Suddenly the wind picked up again, bringing rain in fast-moving sheets across the cove. Before he could get to shelter in the cabin, Abe's clothes were almost as wet as those of the men who had jumped into the river. He

81

shivered as he undressed and put on his spare long winter underwear. He hung his wet clothing on the bunk sides. Abe felt sorry for the men out on the deck, and wondered if getting soaking wet was often part of a boatman's life. He felt lucky to have a bunk in the cabin, even if the thin mattress made the bed almost as hard as the floor.

He thought perhaps he'd have trouble going to sleep because of the slant of the bed, but he never knew when Barney's snores began. Suddenly he was being awakened in the first gray light of a December Sunday.

"Hit the deck, Matey." Barney was speaking very quietly to keep from awakening Mr. Lagrande, who slept just beyond the curtain. Abe blinked several times and rubbed his eyes to get himself awake enough to start his first full day of work.

Before Abe was out on the deck in his still damp dungarees, Barney was in the water again to make the needed repair. The damaged plank was now above the water-line and in the light of early morning the damage could be seen clearly.

Paul, the cook, had kept the firewood reasonably dry with a canvas cover, and he and Abe managed to get a fire started to fix a hot meal for the crew and passengers. Before the bacon and cornbread were ready, Barney yelled, "Abe, send the tar bucket down on a line and fix me a couple of feet of oakum."

Leaning over the gunwales as he lowered the bucket and a length of twisted oakum, Abe could see Barney forcing a plank end back into position, just above the water line, and heard him call out, "Cap'n, this plank will hold with a couple of pegs. 'Tain't split through." Two other men, George and Josh, were now with Barney in the water, one with a mallet and wooden pegs in hand and the other with a hand turned drill and bit.

The sun came up over the low hills across the river to the east, all signs of the storm now gone. By the time the repair work was finished, a gentle breeze promised a warmer than usual early winter day, one that would help dry the men's clothing. The *Rosalie* was eased back into the deeper water of the cove to see if the repair would hold, while the men had a delayed breakfast. Abe, sharing in the work, felt that he was now a working member of the crew.

In the afternoon, there was a stop of an hour or two at the French village of Saint Genevieve, the first settlement on the west bank of the Mississippi, built as a shipping point for lead from nearby mines. The *Rosalie* was to take on some lead, her last cargo for the voyage. Abe, as clerk, went with the captain to write the bill of lading for a half ton of lead "pigs."

Afterwards he delivered a small sack of mail to the Saint Genevieve postmaster, and then was free from other duties while the lead was brought on board and stowed below in the hold. While they waited for the captain's return, Abe and Toni worked some more on her English. Abe tried to think of good words to teach her.

"You have *père*—papa?" Toni asked, as Abe hesitated. She pointed toward her father, now relaxing with a book, on the other side of the deck.

Abe took the cue. He would teach her family names. "Yes, Toni. My "papa" is my father. Say it, please."

Toni obliged. Abe went on. "Sometimes an American boy or girl calls the father of the family Dad or Daddy, or—like you, papa or just pa. I have two sisters. Girls, like you. I have a sister named Hannah, and I have a sister named Rachel."

Toni tried out these words. "Sister Hannah. Sister Rachel. I will know Hannah and Rachel when we come back." After a moment she asked, "You have *maman? Mère?*"

"*Mère?* Oh, you mean do I have a mother. Mo-ther. Say it, Toni."

"Mo-ther. *Mère* is mo-ther."

"That's right, Toni. Father, mother, sister, brother—that makes a family."

Toni repeated the words and started the list again. But this time when she said, "Mother," her voice changed. Abe looked at her and saw that there were tears in her eyes.

"Oh, Toni! I do not mean to make you cry. What's the matter?"

When Toni had wiped her eyes with the pretty handkerchief she drew from the little silk bag she carried, she tried to smile. She saw how upset Abe looked, and said, "You did not make me cry, Abraham. You are good boy. I cry when I think of my mother. I love her very much, but she is gone. In France. She die."

"Oh, Toni, I am so sorry." Clumsily, he reached out and patted her shoulder. She looked up and smiled. "We

84

go on, Abraham. We go on learn English—some happy words."

They stood for a moment looking out at the river, watching a flatboat slowly approaching.

"What word for *bateau?*" Toni asked as the flatboat drew closer.

"Boat will do. They call that kind a flatboat because that's what it is. Flat, like a big box." Abe gestured with his hands to give the idea of the box-like shape of the flatboat.

As the flatboat floated past the *Rosalie,* Abe was startled to hear his name called.

"Hey, Carson! Why don'tcha get a faster boat?"

There, standing on the roof that covered the back half of the flatboat was a familiar figure. Gus! He was holding one of the sweeps, a side oar that was a long pole with a board attached to the end in the water, much like the *Rosalie's* rudder.

Abe was still trying to think of something to call back to Gus when there was sudden trouble on the flatboat. It looked as if the boxy craft might have had a bad bump from a snag.

"You, GUS!" one of the men yelled and swore loudly. "Mind your sweep, you green horn!"

Gus had suddenly fallen backwards as the boat lurched, lifting the sweep from the water as he fell. He was scrambling to get to his feet and get the oar back into the water as the boat moved on.

Toni was laughing as she said, "That mean boy! He look funny, is it not?"

Abe grinned at her. "Yeah—I mean, yes, Toni. Likely we'll see old Gus again. A keelboat like the *Rosalie* can go down the river much faster because of the way she's made. But sometimes the flatboat men just let the boat drift on down the river at night, and they catch up with a boat like ours when we make our stops. Even so, we'll pass her again."

Toni's eyes had a puzzled look. "Why you call a boat she like a girl? In France, *bateau* is he, like a boy!"

Abe stared at her, puzzled. "She is? I mean, he is?" He pushed back his stocking cap and scratched his head. "You got me, Toni. I mean, I don't know. Let's ask Barney."

Barney paused a moment before he called down to them, "Don't rightly know why. But I think it's 'cause a boat can be as ornery as a woman, when she has a mind to."

Abe saw that Toni looked as puzzled as before. "Orn-ornery?" she asked.

"Never mind, Toni. You wouldn't like Barney's answer, anyway. You can call *Rosalie* a he, if you want to."

"English—he is funny!" said Toni, and her eyes were laughing as she looked at Abe.

That ended the English lessons for the day. Captain Byrne came back on board and Abe had book work to do for him as the *Rosalie* continued her voyage. Abe, no longer seeing the drawing of the lady that he had seen on

Sunday, asked, "Captain, who was the pretty lady in that picture I saw yesterday?"

Abe was startled to see the same look on Captain Byrne's face that had come over him when he saw the printed sheet that Abe had pulled out from under the bunk, as if he remembered something very upsetting. "I-I didn't mean to ask something wrong—" Abe stammered. A few seconds went by and the captain was silent. Abe was sure he must be angry.

When the captain spoke, his voice sounded as if he was fighting back tears. "It's all right, Abraham." More silence, and then he said in a more normal voice, "We have work to do. Get the ledger and open it to the Bill of Lading page."

The entrees were soon made for the shipments of shot and lead, and the costs of the purchases also recorded. "That's probably the last entry you'll need to make until we are almost to New Orleans and start delivering goods. Close the ink bottle tight so the ink won't dry up."

Abe blotted the page carefully and closed the ledger. "Anything else I should do, Captain?" he asked. There was no answer, and when he turned back from the table Captain Byrne was gone. When he went out and up to the roof, he saw that Barney was handling the rudder and Mike was on watch in Barney's usual post. Abe walked back to speak to Barney.

"I think I made the captain angry, Barney, but I didn't mean to. I just asked him about the picture I saw on the desk yesterday. It was of a pretty lady. And he seemed kind of bothered a few days ago when I pulled out a piece of heavy paper that was stuck between the boards. I think he likes me all right, but I wish I knew more about him, so I wouldn't upset him."

Barney was quiet for a moment. Then he said, "Something happened that bothers him, Matey. Guess I could tell you a little about it. I have known him since we worked together when St. Louis and all the land on the west bank of the river belonged to Spain. New Orleans and the land around it was still Spanish land, too. Maybe you learned that the United States didn't get all that land until eight years ago, in 1803. Spain had to give it back to France just before that, and we bought it from France. Follow me, lad?"

"Yes, sir. We learned in school about that and how Captain Lewis and Captain Clark went exploring up the Missouri River—and how the fur trade for St. Louis really grew then."

"Well, while it was still Spanish land the American boat owners had a hard time 'cause Spain wouldn't let them go down to New Orleans to sell their cargo. Going down the rivers—the Ohio and the Mississippi—was the only way for the people who lived west of the Alleghenies—western Pennsylvania, Kentucky, Tennessee—to sell their crops and other stuff. Jonathan Byrne had a flatboat then, and I worked with him. So some of the boat owners got together and figured a way to do it. They found out that a boat owner could pretend he was really Spanish and be allowed to take his goods to New Orleans where the owners of ocean ships would buy the stuff and take it to the cities to sell." Barney stopped talking and looked sharply at Abe.

"Now comes the secret—and you gotta promise me you won't let on to the captain if I tell you about it." Barney's voice was stern.

Abe nodded and crossed his heart with his fingers, "I promise, for sure, Barney."

"Don't ever forget and tell someone! That's what that paper you found was about. Same as some other boat owners did, he got that paper. Says he's a citizen of Spain. He only did it 'cause he wanted to sell his goods and have money to get married." Barney stopped talking and looked quickly at Abe. "Forget I told you that, Matey. He's as American as you and me, and he'll fight to stop England from taking our country back. Guess you've heard about the war that's likely to start soon with England—England wants to take the Mississippi back again, and maybe all the land—including St. Louis. That's what they tell us, anyway—and Cap'n could be arrested for treason, maybe—like happened to Aaron Burr a couple of years ago. Maybe not—but his secret worries him."

Barney turned and looked directly into Abe's eyes. "Cross your heart again and promise me you won't let on to the captain that I told you this! Maybe I shouldn't have...."

Abe looked steadily into Barney's blue eyes as he said, "I promise I won't let on that I know, Barney. I really do—'cause you're my best friend on this boat!"

"That I am, Matey. Cap'n's a good man. You do right by him and don't ask him any questions that might upset him. Don't ask him about the lady in the picture, neither.

89

That's his other secret, and I'm not a-gonna tell you about her."

Abe said, "I won't ask him again, Barney. But Spain doesn't own New Orleans any more! It's American now. So doesn't that make Captain Byrne an American?"

Barney shrugged his shoulders. "Always was, far as I'm concerned. Now you better go back down 'cause it's gettin' dark and we're choosin' a place for the night. Git goin', Matey!"

Darkness came early those December afternoons and the sun was already below the treetops along the western bank. Soon the crew was busy guiding the boat to a little inlet alongside an island. There they tied the lines to sturdy trees to make the *Rosalie* secure for the night. Paul called Abe to help him as they built a fire on shore and finished cooking the rabbit stew Paul had started in the early afternoon.

One of Abe's duties was to serve meals to Antoinette and Mr. Lagrande. He came back on board to set a table in the gentlemen's cabin, where Toni and her father chose to eat the evening meal instead of going ashore in the chilly evenings as the crew did.

"Bring your plate and come sit with us," Mr. Lagrande said as Abe ladled out stew for him and Antoinette.

"Oh, no sir," Abe replied quickly. "I'm not allowed to do that. I'm supposed to help the cook serve the men and then clean up. But thank you for asking me." He was aware that his voice had gone into that horrible squeak, and felt his face growing hot as he saw Toni smiling up at him. Flustered, he walked backwards as he spoke and found himself suddenly wrapped in the curtain that closed off the cabin.

Grabbing at the curtain, he nearly lost his balance and almost pulled the curtain down. "'Scuse me," was all he could think to say, and he could feel his face burning. He retreated as quickly as possible, angry with himself for being so awkward.

A quick glance as he pulled the curtain closed showed him Toni's smiling face, with those dark eyes that seemed to have a special glow. *She'll think I'm an awful clod!* he thought. He still felt embarrassed when he said goodnight.

The *Rosalie* rode a little deeper in the water because of the added weight of the lead they had taken on at Saint Genevieve. As they started downriver in the morning, Captain Byrne cautioned Barney, "Be extra watchful for snags from here on, Barney. We're carrying a heavy cargo and could get caught on a planter that's only a couple of feet under the surface."

Barney nodded agreement. "Sure will keep an eye open for 'em, Cap'n. I think I might teach Abe to know the signs, too. He's got better eyes 'n me."

From then on, when Abe was near and Barney spotted signs of a treacherous snag, he pointed out the way the water parted, the shadowy look—all the signs that could mean danger lurking.

"Watch out fer them sawyers," Barney told him as he pointed to one. "See how it drops down and then comes up, kind of like a man sawing. That's why it's called a sawyer."

Abe soon could tell at a good distance whether they were approaching a sawyer or a planter just from the way each disturbed the water. Sometimes Abe saw the telltale changes before Barney did, to Barney's pleasure. Other times, Abe's attention would wander and he'd get a stern reminder.

"You can't get careless in this kind of water, Matey," Barney said as he signaled danger to Captain Byrne. "You should have seen that one!" he added when the emergency ended.

The day passed without more stops. In mid-morning, Barney pointed out Kaskaskia, a village growing around the remains of an old French fort on the Illinois side. They made nearly forty miles that day, even though there were dangerous eddies and sand bars they had to maneuver around. As darkness came, they tied up at a small pier that belonged to one of the few settlers along the Missouri shore, a Mr. Fenwick.

The owner came down to meet them, carrying a lantern. "Ahoy there, Captain Byrne!" he called. "Come up to my cabin and keep me company this fine winter night."

There was only one set of snores to disturb Abe's sleep that night, and he was up and helping the cook when Captain Byrne came aboard in the early morning.

"Fenwick tells me there's river pirates hanging around near the mouth of the Ohio," the captain told Barney. "He says we should stop at Cape Girardeau tonight, well above the Ohio."

They were soon moving on down the river, while Abe and the cook took care of preparing and serving breakfast.

When that and the cabin cleaning were taken care of, Abe took his place beside Barney, rather hoping to see the pirates the captain had warned them to be watching for.

"Don't think we'll have any pirate trouble, Matey," Barney said. "Likely they're holin' up for the winter about now."

The only interesting thing Abe could see was an eagle flying out of a small cave, far up on a tower-like rock formation in the water near the Illinois bank.

"Devil's Oven, they call that little cave," Barney said. "Lots of places named for Old Satan—all the worst ones along the river, where we have to say our prayers to get through. Devil's Race Ground is one of the worst places— shallow all the way across and loaded with snags, except for a narrow channel where the water rushes like crazy!"

Toni had been listening. "What is it that you mean, devil?" she asked Abe. He was trying to explain when their attention was caught by another rock formation, even taller than the one that held Devil's Oven. They had to steer around this rock tower, for it was in the middle of the channel they were following.

"Grand Tower. Deep water between it and the shore," Barney explained, "but terrible dangerous. Could hit rocks there. So we play it safe and stay clear of that rock."

Toni said, "It old Devil Rock Tower, *n'est-ce pas?*"

"Right you are, Miss Antoinette," Barney agreed.

The cook had the wild turkey roasting all that morning, and they feasted on it at noon. Abe couldn't remember anything ever tasting better, even his mother's roasts. After his work with the cook was finished, he and Toni had another English lesson.

That night they stopped at the village of Cape Girardeau, and by the next day, Wednesday, Abe began to feel he was an experienced member of the *Rosalie's* crew. He was of help to Barney several times when his young eyes spotted dangerous snags before the older man saw them.

The sun was setting when they reached a stretch of winding river with one turn after another. As they began to round a bend that blocked the view of all but a few feet of river, Barney said, "They call this the Grand Turn, Abe. It's a bad place for snags. Look as far ahead as you can while we round it."

"Good work, Matey," Barney said after Abe had spotted a snag before he had seen it himself. "Best we find a place to tie up for the night. Bad water ahead. We need good light. Tomorrow morning we'll really see a lot of water pouring into Old Man River, 'cause we'll pass the mouth of the Ohio."

Abe and Toni were both on the deck the next day watching for the first view of the "beautiful Ohio." And there it was, broad and with gently sloping banks. They had left the highest bluffs along the Mississippi behind, too, and the land was beginning to level off as they moved southward, with only an occasional low bluff.

They hadn't gone very far below the Ohio's mouth when Paul complained to the captain, "Cap'n, we're about out of meat. Can we tie up long enough for Mike and me to hunt? We're down to beans and cornbread until we get us more turkeys or maybe a deer."

Before Captain Byrne answered, he heard someone calling from the left bank of the river. A short distance ahead, there stood four Indians, waving and beckoning for the *Rosalie* to stop. "Maybe we can get meat even faster," he told Paul. "That's Choctaw country over there and usually when we come by, they have some meat ready to sell us. We'll stop just ahead at Wolf Island and find out."

Mr. Lagrande, Toni and Abe were on the forward deck where Abe had been continuing his conversation lessons with Toni. When he heard the order to dock, the lesson had to end. He began unwinding the mooring lines as the crew prepared to stop the boat. Ready to cast the lines, he watched the approach to Wolf Island, the largest island they had seen for many miles.

"Why we stop?" Toni asked. "The sky is blue, not night."

"Look over there," Abe answered, pointing to the left bank. "Some Indians want us to stop."

Toni cried out, "Oh, Abe! Indians kill us! Tell Captain not stop—please!"

Barney heard her frightened voice. He called down, "Not these Indians, Miss Toni. No need to be afraid. See—they are waving to us like old friends! We always buy food from them."

Toni was not yet convinced. Abe noticed that she stood close to her father, clinging to his arm, watching as Captain Byrne got a small sack of gunpowder. Her face showed more worry as he filled another sack with lead shot from one of the kegs they had taken on at Herculaneum.

"Just to pay for meat," Abe said, trying to ease her worry. The skiff was lowered into the water from the aft deck. Barney would go ashore in it with the captain to deal with the Indians.

As the two were getting into the small boat, Mike ran back to the stern, carrying his rifle. "Cap'n, let me go along. Might be a trick and you'll need me and me rifle."

"No, Mike. These are Choctaws—tame as white men. Besides, we'll need the room in the boat for a couple of sides of venison. But take Paul with you and get us some game on shore while we're gone. This is Wolf Island, and it's nigh onto five miles long. Ought to be a turkey or two you might get. We'll stop to pick you up at the far end."

When Captain Byrne and Barney had started toward the shore where the Indians waited, the crew moved the Rosalie around the end of the island to the western side, where there was a good deep channel. When they reached a good place, the lines were tied to trees and the gangplank put in place. Mike and Paul, with knives and the things they needed to fire their rifles hanging from their belts, started into the woods.

From where the boat was docked, the skiff carrying the captain and Barney was out of sight. Abe wanted to go on shore where he could walk around and see how they were doing. He asked, "Want to walk around where we can see what's happening, Toni?"

But Mr. Lagrande answered for his daughter. "I prefer to keep her here with me, Abraham. As you see, she doesn't have proper shoes for walking on this rough ground." As Abe looked at Toni's feet he agreed. She was wearing a pair of thin-soled slippers, tied with cords around her calves, shoes that wouldn't take her through one bramble patch and would certainly pull off in a bit of mud. And she still seemed to be afraid, holding onto her father's hand.

Three of the crew already had fishing lines in the water off the side of the boat. The fourth boatman still on the boat, a fellow named George, went with Abe. The two walked along the bank for about a half mile before they could see the skiff and the two men in it, now at the far shore. Barney was stepping out into the water to pull the boat to a stop and tie it to a tree.

Abe and George watched as Captain Byrne got out and Abe could see that he politely greeted the Indians. With the greetings over, the captain was getting right to business. As Barney picked up what looked like a side of venison and carried it to the boat, Captain Byrne appeared to be counting out lead shot from the pouch he carried into the hands of the leader of the Indian group. A second side of venison was purchased for a sack of gunpowder. They were ready to leave when the Indians stopped them. "More!" they cried and brought out two more large turkeys, not yet stripped of their feathers.

George said, "Looks like yer gonna hafta pull a lot of feathers off them birds, Abe."

"I don't mind except when the wind blows the little fluffy ones into my face," Abe said. "I learned how to get chickens, ducks, and even turkeys ready for my mother at home. My pa's a good turkey hunter." Talking about his family brought a sudden wave of homesickness, and Abe turned away from George so he wouldn't see his teary eyes.

Now the captain appeared to be taking a coin from the little bag he wore under his shirt, first turning his back to the Indians as Barney held their attention, examining the turkeys.

"Likely Barney's arguing that there ain't much meat on them birds," George commented. "Keeps them Injuns from seein' where Cap'n keeps his money."

Now the deal appeared to be finished, and Barney and the captain were about to shove the boat back into the river far enough for it to float. It rode a little deeper as they got back in.

"They's startin' back," George said. "Let's head back to the boat."

They had gone just far enough that the skiff was out of sight when there was the sound of gunfire. "Did that sound like it could be from Mike and Paul?" Abe asked. "It didn't sound very far away."

There was another burst of gunfire. This time it echoed from far down the island.

"That'n was likely Mike bringin' down somep'n," George said. "But that first shot sounded like it was awful close to the *Rosalie!* Let's get back thar, boy!"

CHAPTER 8

Perils of the River

The shot echoed, and then there was a scream coming faintly from the direction of the *Rosalie*. Abe cried out, "George, hurry up! Something's wrong! That was Toni!"

Leaving George to make his way a little slower, he charged ahead, running through the brushy growth along the bank as if it were an open path. When he could see the keelboat's stern deck he slowed down to make less noise as he came closer. Something was definitely wrong. He heard Mr. Lagrande saying gruffly, almost shouting, "Toni, get inside!"

Abe felt a moment of relief, knowing that Toni had not been hurt in what was happening. Now he could see the boat clearly. At the head of the gangplank, two men stood, each holding a large pistol and facing the three boatmen who had been fishing.

"Keep them hands up!" one of the gunmen yelled. The boatmen put down their poles and did as ordered. Waving his pistol at Mr. Lagrande, the gunman added, "You, too, mister! Get over thar with them!"

Toni's father took just a moment to look toward the cabin doorway to make sure that Toni was out of sight, and then he crossed the deck to join the boatmen.

River pirates! Abe was sure that must be who they were. Then he thought of George, coming with his rifle. He turned and went silently back around the bend. With a finger on his lips as a signal to George for silence, he stopped him and whispered, "River pirates on the boat. Is your rifle loaded?"

George nodded. Abe had been planning what they might do, and whispered into George's ear. George nodded again. The two moved along the river bank toward the Rosalie, stepping carefully to avoid making noise. As they came alongside the boat, Abe put his finger on his lips again as a signal to the boatmen, Patrick, Charles, and Josh, who had been fishing from the deck. He was sure at least one of them had seen him and George, but they all quickly turned their eyes back to the pirates.

"Whatcha want us to do?" Josh usually spoke in a quiet voice, but now he was shouting. Abe knew it was to help cover any noise he and George might make. He shuffled his feet noisily as he went on, "Don't shoot and we'll get what you want! Cap'n's not here but we know where there's a keg o' shot." Patrick added, "Yeah. Just don't shoot us! Tell us what you want." Charles pretended to get a bad fit of coughing to make more noise to cover the approach of Abe and George.

George held his gun ready to fire as Abe, on hands and knees, crawled up the gangplank. As he reached the top, he was right behind the pirates, their backs toward him. Soundlessly, he reached out and grabbed the legs of the nearest gunman and pulled. The pirate, swearing loudly, fell face down on the deck, his pistol flying out toward the boatmen. The other man swung about, only to find himself facing George's rifle pointing directly at him.

"Drop that pistol or I'll blast yer brains out!" George yelled. "Drop it and git yer hands into the air!"

100

Abe was doing his best to hold onto the legs of the fallen man, who was trying to crawl toward his pistol, but Josh bent down, snatched it and pointed it into the fellow's face. Patrick, who was standing on the other side of the deck, fishing rod in hand, swung out his line toward the pirate who, at George's order, had dropped his pistol and put his hands up. The fishing line, with its sharp hook at the end, wound around the man's upraised arms. The third crewman, Charles, grabbed that fellow's pistol where it had fallen to the deck. He pointed it at its owner.

"Leggo me legs!" the fallen pirate yelled. He tried hard to kick Abe, who almost lost his grip. Mr. Lagrande, seeing the trouble Abe was having, hurried over and put one foot in its polished boot on the man's back.

"Ow!" the pirate cried out as Mr. Lagrande dug the heel of his boot into the fellow's spine. "Let us go! We'uns won't bother ye none!"

"You can bet me boots you won't bother us no more," Patrick said as he came up behind the man facing George's rifle. He seized the end of a coiled rope that lay on the deck. Charles pulled the man's arms down, and Patrick wrapped the line around his wrists behind his back. The man tried to pull his arms back to raise himself. Josh roughly seized his wrists and held them behind his back. He shouted gleefully, "Here's the other one, Patrick! Bring the line to tie him up!"

"Ow! Lemme go!" the man yelled, raising his head.

Lagrande's answer was to jerk the pirate's head down, face onto the deck. *"Fermez la bouche!"* he shouted.

101

Whether or not he understood French, the man got the idea and closed his mouth.

"Well done, Abraham!" Lagrande said. "You can let go now, before you get a bad kick. He's not going to be able to get up until we let him."

Abe got to his feet and rubbed his sore knees. He looked toward the cabin doorway just in time to glimpse Toni peeking out—and holding the captain's pistol pointed at the standing pirate, who was still facing George's rifle.

"Mr. Lagrande, look at Toni!" Abe said, his voice tense.

Mr. Lagrande, still keeping his foot on the pirate's back, said, *"O, mon dieu!* Abe, take my place!" He hurried over to take the pistol from Toni. Abe, now with his foot on the pirate's back, could hear a rapid spurt of French words from the cabin, and knew that the father was more frightened than he had been by the pirates' attack, frightened for his courageous daughter who knew nothing about guns.

"What's going on?"

It was Captain Byrne's voice. The skiff had pulled up to the stern of the *Rosalie,* and Barney was already out and tying it to an iron ring on the keelboat.

"We sure enough caught us a couple o' big fish, Cap'n," Patrick announced. He turned and waved toward George and Abe. "Course them two had a little to do with it—"

Captain Byrne's reply was a grunt, but Abe saw the twinkle in his eye as he said, nodding his head toward the pirates, "We'll put your catch to dry for a while and get underway as soon as we get this meat on board. You—Josh and Charles—cut enough line to tie these fellows to a couple of stout trees to hold them. George, you keep the rifle aimed while we get this scum off the boat. Patrick, help Barney bring the meat on board."

Abe glanced toward the cabin doorway and there was Toni, her eyes wide and seeming blacker than ever. Her father stood behind her, his hands on her shoulders, as he gave her orders in French to stay where she was.

It was a busy time then. Mr. Lagrande helped Josh and Charles get the fallen man to his feet after they had cut two good lengths of rope. When that one was safely bound to a tree on shore, the other was also escorted to the island woods. George kept his rifle aimed at him until the rope held him firmly to a tree at some distance from his partner. Both of the pirates' pistols were turned over to Captain Byrne.

"Souvenirs of an exciting afternoon," the captain said and took them into his cabin. "It's safe for you to come outside now, Miss Antoinette," he added. "Just think what good stories you'll be able to tell your friends!"

Toni smiled a bit wanly and came onto the deck. Abe noticed that she held onto her father's arm the whole time the men were loading the venison and turkey meat on board, until at last the *Rosalie* was underway. Then she came to stand beside Abe, whose heart was still pounding from all the excitement.

Abe frowned as he said, "Toni, seeing you with that pistol was scarier than grabbing the pirate!"

"I not want you to get hurt," she said.

"Well, don't ever do that again. You've never learned how to use a gun, and if that pistol had gone off—I hate to think what might have happened!"

There was silence for a moment and then Toni reached out and touched Abe's arm. "You *très* brave, Abraham," she said.

Abe felt himself blush. "Aw-w, not so brave. I was plenty scared—afraid the man wouldn't fall. Good thing George was there with his loaded rifle."

George overheard Abe and grinned sheepishly. "You know what, Abe? After it was all over, I saw that I hadn't finished loading—there was no shot in there. If I had to shoot, the rifle'd only have made a big bang and hurt me more'n anyone else!"

"How they get free?" As the boat glided along in the channel, following alongside the island, Toni was looking back at the woods where the men were tied.

Abe said, "Don't worry about them! Likely they're tryin' now to get free and cussin' us all the time. It'll take a while, but they'll loosen the ropes enough to get at least one hand out, and soon they'll be headin' back to their camp in the woods." He looked at Toni's face, with her brow drawn into worry lines. "We'll be well beyond this island then, too far for them to try to get even with us. But I don't think they'll forget this day very soon. And neither will I."

At the foot of the island, the *Rosalie* slowed almost to a stop, pulled close to the shore where Mike and Paul were waiting. They had two more wild turkeys and three big rabbits to add to the meat supply, and a lot of questions about what had been going on.

There was plenty of work for Abe then, helping Paul and getting ready for the evening meal. They tied up at an island about ten miles farther down the river.

As they were eating supper, Captain Byrne said, "Tomorrow we should get to New Madrid. It's about thirty miles from here. I have some business to take care of there. We'll spend tomorrow night there, and maybe the next night, too."

But that was not to be.

Things began as usual in the morning, except that skies were gray and the breeze was cold and damp. Abe felt the chill as he went on deck to help Paul. He pulled his new stocking cap down over his ears.

"More wood, Abe," Paul said. He was busy baking corn cakes as he spoke.

Abe didn't answer, nor did he go to the stacked wood chunks. He stood gazing out at the bank off to the right. The willow trees formed a thick screen, as they did along most of the river banks. He yawned. *Wish I could sleep late for once. Maybe I'm not supposed to be a boatman after all. Seems like we've been on this river forever and it's not even a week since we left Saint Louis.* He turned toward Paul. To his surprise, Paul was glaring at him, with his hands on his hips.

"I told you to get me some more wood! Stop mooning around and earn your keep, boy."

"Oh—I didn't hear you, Paul. Sorry." Abe pushed his cap up a bit to uncover his ears, and hurried to get the wood. As he fed it to the fire, he muttered, "Guess I'm not much help this morning. How near are we to New Orleans, Paul?"

Paul was turning the corncakes over on the makeshift griddle. He paused a moment to give Abe a questioning look. "You sure ain't used to the river, are you, boy? We've only come one week. Got weeks to go before we get anywhere near New Orleans!"

Barney called down, "Matey, bring my cakes up here to me. We've got a big bend comin' right soon."

"Yes, sir, soon as I get some to the captain," Abe called back.

Captain Byrne was just coming down the ladder, having put Mike on duty manning the rudder sweep. He took his tin mug of strong coffee and plate of corn cakes and bacon inside to his cabin, and Abe headed up the ladder with Barney's breakfast.

"Hold on a bit until we get her pulled off to the left to get around this old willow island that's right in the bend," Barney said. "Channel's off that way."

"How do you know which side of the island to go on?" Abe asked. "Looks the same on both sides to me."

"I'll show you later. Come back up here when Paul doesn't need your help." As Abe started toward the ladder, Barney took a swallow of coffee from his mug, shuddered and said, "Ugh! That's strong enough to grow back my head of hair!"

Abe grinned at Barney. Then he went down to the deck to finish getting breakfast to the crew. When he had time to eat, he took one swallow of the strong coffee to help him feel warmer. That was enough for him. He thought longingly of breakfast at home, where the corn cakes were tender and his mug of milk cold and fresh.

He had time then, since Toni and her father were not yet up, to go back to Barney's roost on the roof. They had rounded the bend and were approaching another island. This time Barney was signaling for the boat to head for a channel on the right.

"Heard you asking how far to New Orleans, Matey," he said. "Here, take over the watch for a minute and I'll show you where we are." He reached into his jacket pocket to pull out a well-worn small book.

"This here's called *The Navigator*. It's a guide book for boatmen on the Ohio and the Mississippi." He turned to a page with a map on it. The river was shown as a black twisting ribbon, with a gray line running down through it, like a long snake in the river. "That line is to show the best channel," he said, and handed the open book to Abe. "Here, you take it and find Wolf Island where we had the pirate set-to."

He chuckled as he went back to watching the water ahead. To dodge a planter, he signaled for a slight turn. "Just wonderin' how long it took them two to get free o' them ropes." He glanced at Abe and added, "You can borry the book for a little later on, and figure out how far it is to New Orleans. Right now we've got to get around Island Number 8. See it on the map?"

"Yup, there it is!" Abe said. "Looks like we've got another big bend coming. This sure is a twisty old river."

"Ye're right on that point, Matey. And that bend's a bad 'un. I see the passengers are up. Go tend to them now, and come back as soon as you're through. Got about four miles to go alongside this island, but this afternoon I'll sure like your help. We've got a dandy comin' up."

Abe tucked the book back into Barney's pocket. "When we've got easy going, I'll find out about New Orleans," he said as he went down the ladder.

"Good morning, Abraham," Toni said.

"*Bon matin,* Antoinette. See, I'm learning French from you, Toni. That was right for 'good morning,' wasn't it?"

Toni clapped her hands. "Very good, Abraham. And you were very good yesterday, too."

Abe blushed. "Aw, just lucky those guys didn't hear me sneakin' up on 'em." Again that squeaky voice! Hurriedly, he went to get breakfast plates for them. "I guess you'll want to eat in the cabin this morning. It's kind of chilly out here."

When he had left them to eat their breakfast, Paul put him to work on skinning the rabbits, something Abe had done often at home. He was busy all the rest of the morning. It was mid-afternoon when he had a chance to go back up to the roof. To the left was another of the many "willow islands" in the river.

"You're just in time, Matey," Barney said. "I want you to keep a close watch on the river. We're coming into a bad bend, and there's a big old island smack in the middle

108

of the river—Number 10 on the map." He pulled the guidebook from his pocket. "Here, look it up—near the page where a corner's bent down."

Abe soon found the map, and Island Number 10. "Looks like the shortest way is to go to the right, Barney."

"Right channel's shorter, like you said, but we're apt to get hung up in it. Water's low and the river's shallower on the right. That means we have to take the left channel and watch out for a sandbar. We'll have to hug the shore on the left to be sure of having deep enough water. Ho— look, there's a nasty planter!" He signaled to the captain to pull a bit to the right.

"One thing you'll learn, Matey," he went on, "there's almost always sandbars forming in sharp bends like this one, and we'll have to get on over to the left bank. Real bad sandbars along this island, and got to hug the riverbank around the curve, like the guidebook says."

The two of them were busy watching for snags as they approached the big bend with the island in mid-river just ahead. The captain, back at the rudder, was kept busy working to miss the planter and then get closer to the left bank.

They were watching the water just ahead intently when a yell from the captain took them by surprise. "Flatboat ahead! Looks like it's hung up on the bar! Back her, men! Stand to your poles!"

"Oh, my sainted mother!" Barney cried out. "She's hung up on that sandbar alongside the island! Down we go, Abe, where we can help back us away. Grab an oar!"

As they took up oars, the other six men were already working with the poles, using them to act as brakes against the current's push downriver. Three men worked on the running boards on each side of the cabin, frantically trying to push the *Rosalie* away from the big flatboat as the river pushed her toward it.

Every crewman was busy, leaning hard against a pole when Barney shouted to the captain, "I'll start warping!"

He seized the loose end of the cordelle, which was wound around a capstan near the prow, between the oarsmen's seats. He called to Abe, "Unreel the line for me and keep her unreeling until I get this end around a tree. Then tighten her up and start winding!"

By the time he finished his orders, Barney had already gone over the "gunnels" and into the water, heading upstream. Abe put down his oar and did as he was told, seeing that the line continued to unwind from the capstan as Barney, with the end of the cordelle over his shoulder, swam until he reached the shore. Dripping wet, he scrambled up the bank and through the willow tree brush toward a large tree upriver about one hundred feet.

A minute later Abe saw Barney wind the rope around the tree. The cordelle was still unwinding, letting the boat continue to go with the current, when Barney yelled, "Reel her in!"

Abe tried to reverse the turn of the pole handle at the top of the capstan, but it kept on unwinding. The current, still pushing the boat downstream, was stronger than Abe.

Patrick, nearest of the men with poles, came running to help Abe. "Here we go, me lad!" He leaned against the handle, and slowly, with a creaking sound, it began to rewind the rope, working against the river's current.

Patrick needed all the room available to push against the capstan handle. "Out o' me way, lad, and I can wind her faster," he said. And Abe stepped clear. There was a sudden thud and a creaking of the line as the prow of the boat began to swing out from the shore, pushing in a circle toward the flatboat. But it still looked as if the *Rosalie's* stern would surely strike the back corner of the flatboat.

"Starboard with the poles!" Captain Byrne yelled. "Push, men, push!"

Feeling a bit useless, Abe watched as the boat's stern came closer and closer to the flatboat. *How can I ever do what these men do?* he wondered. *I'll never be really worth my salt around here!* He stood watching, feeling useless, as the *Rosalie* came closer and closer to the flatboat. *Will we crash? Surely the skiff, still "in tow," will also be smashed to bits.* And then, with only an inch to spare, the *Rosalie* responded to the pull of the cordelle and the push of the poles against the river bottom. She cleared the flatboat's corner, skiff and all. On the foredeck, Patrick was rewinding the cordelle faster as the current had less push against the side of the *Rosalie*. A minute or two later Barney's call came for a mooring line to be thrown to him. The keelboat was about fifty feet in the clear.

"That was close, boys!" Captain Byrne called. "Not more than an inch between us—but keep leaning on those poles so the current doesn't get us back downriver before we can get better mooring."

On the island, the flatboat crew of four men were wiping their brows with big bandanna kerchiefs. They were sweating both from exhaustion at laboring to free their boat from the sandbar and from fear of a collision.

"Gimme a hand, Patrick," said Barney. The warping line was around his waist as he climbed back aboard at the gangplank opening. The captain joined Patrick in hoisting a dripping Barney onto the forward deck. As Barney untied the warping line, Patrick rewound it onto the captstan in readiness for the next emergency.

There was still the matter of the flatboat blocking the channel, too narrow at that point for safe entrance by another craft. Captain Byrne called out, "You—George, Mike, Charles—take your poles and get in the skiff. See if you can help them get that old tub free before another boat comes along and wrecks us all. Seems to be just a front corner that's hung up. Maybe just shifting the cargo will make a difference."

Abe, looking back at the flatboat, saw a familiar figure. Sure enough, there was Gus, looking as if he'd rather be anywhere else.

"Halloo, Gus!" Abe called. "Why don'tcha get a faster boat?"

CHAPTER 9

Terror in the Night

George, Mike and Charles, taking their poles with them in the skiff, beached the small boat. They were soon standing in the water on the sandbar, joining the efforts of the four men of the flatboat crew, using their poles as pry bars to try to lift the boat loose. Even though it was mid-December, they all had to stop to wipe sweat from rolling into their eyes. But for all their hard labor, the flatboat hadn't budged an inch.

Abe, on board the *Rosalie,* was helping Paul cut venison steaks for the men's supper. When he had a free minute, he went toward the stern to see what was going on at the flatboat. Before he got there he heard a loud splash, followed by Gus's voice, high and whiny, swearing.

An angry Gus had thrown his pole into the water. Abe saw him turn to his crewmates, folding his arms over his chest defiantly. He shouted, "This ain't gonna help none. We'uns are just wearin' ourselves out for nothin'!" Then, leaving his pole in the water, he climbed the bank to the island.

Barney was on the stern deck. "Barney, look who's first to quit!" Abe said. "That's the way Gus always was when there was hard work to be done!" Gus had turned his back on the tired men and was walking toward the island's woods.

Everyone still on the keelboat heard the flatboat captain swear loudly. Then he yelled, "Get back to work, you no good loafer! And get that pole out of the water!" Gus hesitated a moment and then shrugged his shoulders defiantly. Abe was sure he was considering desertion. But just then a wildcat's yowl reached them from the woods. Gus sauntered back, waded into the water and retrieved his pole.

Toni, her father, and Captain Byrne were also out watching the rescue work. Toni said, "Oh, Papa, I do not like that boy Gus at all!"

Captain Byrne muttered, "Glad I didn't take that lazy lout on my boat." Then he said, "Barney, get over there and start lightening her."

"Aye, Cap'n. We'll do that." Barney was still wet from his trip to shore with the cordelle, so he waded and swam the short distance to the flatboat. Soon the *Rosalie* men were hoisting boxes and barrels from the forward deck, pushing them down the gangplank to the flatboat men on the shore. A scowling Gus was among them. When about twenty of the heavy pieces of cargo had been moved ashore, the forward part of the flatboat rose an inch or two.

"Ready to try shoving again?" Barney called to the flatboat captain. Again the men took up the poles to pry the boat loose. At last, after much labor and time lost, the flatboat was freed. The men of the Rosalie pushed their skiff into the water and headed back to their boat, leaving the work of keeping the flatboat afloat and reloading it to her crew.

Abe heard Paul calling him, but took one last look to see what was going on at the flat-boat. It had been moved a few more feet from the sandbar and the crew was busy returning the heavy freight to the deck. Gus and another man were pushing a heavy barrel up the plank, obviously finding it hard labor. Abe grinned in satisfaction as he started back to the foredeck. As he turned, he hollered, "Atta boy, Gus! You can do it!"

At hearing Abe's voice, Gus let go his end of the barrel and raised his arm to make an obscene gesture at Abe; the barrel rolled back. Gus's partner cursed and the captain shouted gruffly, "You, Gus! Keep a-pushin'! You're a no-good—" and the string of names he called Gus was lost in the breeze as Abe made his way back to the foredeck.

By then the sun had set. Darkness would soon make further travel dangerous. With his crew back on board and ready to eat the evening meal, Captain Byrne looked about uneasily. He spoke to Barney. "We can't stay where we are now, Barney. Look at how little space there is for another boat to get by us. If another one comes down the river, there'll be a collision. I think we should bushwhack her a little farther up the river, and tie up for the night."

Overhearing the captain's words, Abe wondered just what Captain Byrne meant for the crew to do. *What is bushwhacking?* He soon found out. The boat was poled close to the shore which was lined with bushes and low willow branches hanging over the water. Barney went ashore, ready to move the mooring line to another tree as the boat was moved upstream.

The men, even Paul the cook, stood in a line on the starboard side, facing the shore where bushes and willow

115

saplings grew. Each of them reached as far ahead as he could to grab the bushes or hanging branches. Holding the bush clump or sapling, they all pulled at the same time. As the boat moved ahead, each man took hold of the next bush. They soon had the *Rosalie* far enough up the river to be safe. As the men held the *Rosalie* in place, the captain cast out the aft mooring line for Barney to secure her for the night. Then, at last, Paul and Abe could hand out the plates with the overcooked steaks.

Some of the men grumbled about the flatboat crew's spoiling their dinner, but they were too tired to do much more, and all retired early. The captain's goal of reaching New Madrid that day was short of accomplishment by twelve miles.

Paul and Abe were preparing breakfast the next morning when the *Rosalie,* getting an early start, passed the flatboat. It was tied to a tree on the island, safely below the sandbar, the cargo back on board. The crew of four was stretched out on the cabin roof, sound asleep.

"I think the one with the loudest snore is old Gus," Abe remarked. Out of mercy to Gus' exhausted crew mates, Abe resisted the impulse to shout, "Wake up, Gus!" as they passed. Another river bend put the flatboat out of sight.

Barney was too busy helping the captain guide the boat safely through the treacherous channel to come down from the roof for breakfast. Abe took his breakfast up to him. "Want me to do watch now?" the boy asked.

"Hold it for a bit, Matey. We've got the rest of this loop in Old Man River to finish. Then he straightens out and we go right down the middle to New Madrid, where Cap'n wants to stop."

"How far is that?"

"'Bout ten more miles, and no big islands to get by."

Abe, paging through *The Navigator,* figured that after they reached Natchez there would be nearly three–hundred miles still to go to New Orleans. *Seems like we've been gone from St. Louis for months already,* he mused. Looking ahead, he could see only the endless twists and bends.

When Barney finished eating, Abe went down to see about the passengers' needs. Later in the morning, when the *Rosalie* was almost taking care of herself in the long, straight run before New Madrid, Captain Byrne told him to check the mail sacks for mail to be delivered to the New Madrid post office.

They would dock at a creek mouth just above the village and remain there for the rest of the day and all night. It was Saturday, one week from the day the trip started. Now at last the six men of the crew could have a few hours of freedom. The captain and Barney would need to use this last opportunity to get supplies. There were no more towns where they could shop until they had gone seven–hundred and fifty miles more, to Natchez. And they had come only one hundred thirty miles from St. Louis this first week!

Seems like we'll never get there! Abe thought.

As they prepared to tie up at the creek at the north edge of New Madrid, Captain Byrne warned them that they'd be making a very early start on Sunday morning to get well beyond Little Prairie by night. Little Prairie was a very small village about thirty miles down the Mississippi from New Madrid.

"Do as you please until sundown," he told the crew. "But at sundown the gangplank will be pulled in, and everyone should be back on board."

Abe had found a small amount of mail for New Madrid and set the sack on deck next to the cabin doorway. He expected to find Toni out there to talk with for a few minutes before he helped Paul get the noon meal ready. But Toni was nowhere in sight, although her father was on the bench where he usually sat, reading.

"Where is Toni, sir?" Abe asked. "I haven't seen her since breakfast."

Mr. Lagrande set his book aside. "She seems to be a little unhappy today, Abraham. She did a little mending on one of my shirts this morning, but she said she'd just stay in her bunk afterwards. I'll see if she will come out. Perhaps you can cheer her up a bit."

"Why is she sad today?" Abe asked. "She seemed to be feeling fine yesterday evening. I hope I didn't say anything that hurt her feelings—"

Mr. Lagrande said, "No, Abraham. It was on this day, December 14, 1810—one year ago today—that we lost Antoinette's dear mother. She is thinking of that, I am sure. She loved her mother dearly, and she misses her very much." He saw the distressed look on Abe's face as he rose from the bench. "Don't worry yourself about it, Abraham." He touched the boy's shoulder as he went by. "If you were not on this boat, I am sure the long voyage would be terrible for her!"

When Toni came out onto the deck with her father, Abe saw that her eyes were puffy and reddened. *She's been crying,* he thought. But Toni smiled as she joined him.

"Your father told me why you were sad today," Abe said.

Toni's eyes filled with tears again.

"Oh, Toni, I didn't mean to make you cry!"

"No, Abraham. It is not you. I miss my mother very much. And on the boat there is no woman at all—only men. And you."

"My sister Hannah wanted to come on the boat, but my mother wouldn't let her," Abe said. "We have Uncle Daniel and Aunt Mattie in New Orleans, and she could visit there. She would have been good company for you, Toni—another girl."

"Oh, yes! That would be nice. If only another girl or even a lady could be on the boat, I would not be so—so *solitaire.* How I say it, Abe?"

"I think you mean lonesome, or lonely."

Toni repeated the words.

After several minutes of silence, Abe said, "We are almost to New Madrid. Paul says we will eat on land for a change, if we want to, alongside the creek where we're going to dock, just above the town."

"Creek? What is a creek?" Toni asked.

"Like a river, but not wide." Abe spread out his arms to indicate the breadth of a river, and drew his hands close together to express the narrowness of a creek. "The Mississippi is wide, a creek is narrow."

119

The captain called out orders for docking, and Abe left Toni with her father. It took some careful handling of the keelboat to enter the creek mouth, for the current was like a whirlpool there. They had to go below the creek mouth and then move into it in a hurry, pushed by the swirling current. When the *Rosalie* was moored, Abe helped Paul get the food ready.

When he served Toni and Mr. Lagrande on the creek bank, which rose behind them to the low bluff on which the town was located, Abe asked what the passengers were going to do on their afternoon in town.

"Perhaps we can find a cobbler who will have a pair of sturdier shoes for Antoinette before we must come back to the boat," Mr. Lagrande said. "She might also like to look in the shops for something to do while we are on this long voyage, perhaps some bit of needlework."

When the food was all cleared away, Abe got the mail sack and climbed the path up the bluff to the town. He saw Mr. Lagrande and Toni going into a shop on the first street above the river, a shop with a boot-shaped sign hanging over the door. Abe hoped that the cobbler would be able to fit Toni with some shoes such as his sisters wore in winter.

He found the post office in one of the two main stores, and delivered the sack of mail. "Are you from Captain Jonathan Byrne's boat?" the postmaster-storekeeper asked.

"Yes, sir."

"A fine man. Perhaps he'll look in on us before you move on. But I'm sure he would appreciate your taking our mail that's to go to Natchez and New Orleans," the postmaster said. He emptied the sack and put into it two small bundles of mail before handing it back to Abe.

With the sack over his shoulder, Abe wandered about the town for a while. There was one more general store, a few shops like the cobbler's, and a tavern. There were log buildings on the other streets, mostly small cabins, with gardens behind them with the summer's cornstalks still standing, dry and rattling in the wind. It seemed to Abe that the wind was getting colder.

Walking past the houses, Abe thought about his own family's log house and garden. He wondered if he was missed very much, now that he had been gone a week and a day. Suddenly, he felt sad, and when a dog that looked much like his Towser barked at him, he was so homesick that he decided to go back to the boat. Back on the street nearest the river, he saw Barney, Paul and Captain Byrne going into a store, but he didn't hail them.

Some of the crew, George and Mike, were on guard duty on the *Rosalie*. George was on the foredeck. "Back so soon, Abe? We thought you'd spend the afternoon in the tavern with a mug of ale!"

George meant this to be a joke, but Abe didn't laugh. He just said, "I'll be in my bunk for a while, George, after I put the mail sack in the captain's cabin."

"You sick, Abe?"

"Kinda," Abe answered and entered the cabin. Soon he was stretched out on his bunk. He dozed off after a bit, and dreamed he was back at home. His mother was crying, "Oh, Abraham! I knew something bad would happen!

Look out!" And then the boat was rocking badly, and his mother cried, "Wake up, wake up!"

Someone was shaking his shoulder. But it wasn't his mother. He opened his eyes, and there was Barney, saying, "Wake up, Matey! Time to help Paul."

He struggled to shake off the feeling that his mother was trying to tell him something. He rubbed his eyes, and got down from the bunk, still a bit groggy. Out on the deck, a minute or two later, he saw Toni and her father returning from their afternoon in town.

"Abraham! New shoes! Now I can walk in the woods!"

Toni pulled up her dress skirt just a bit and stood on one foot, pushing the other one forward for Abe to see. The cobbler had fitted her with moccasins with an extra layer of sole leather. Her pleasure was contagious, and Abe felt his spirits lifting. But when he settled on his bunk for the night, his mother's worried face was before his eyes again.

⧗ ⧗ ⧗

They left the creek dockage with the first light of dawn. "No need to stop at Little Prairie," Captain Byrne announced. "We'll go right on as far as we can before dark and tie up at an island a little farther down."

That was the plan they followed, passing more flatboats than usual as they traveled on. Barney explained that the fall harvest was being taken to market while the upper Ohio River was still open, before the treacherous ice formed.

"Lots of corn on those boats, and likely some barrels o' hog meat, too," he said. "Crews will unload at New

Orleans and those flatboats will be broken up and the lumber sold—if they don't hit a sawyer somewhere along the river and break up sooner!"

"How do the crews get back to their families?"

Barney said, "It's a long, long walk—but that's what they do. If home is back at St. Louis, they follow the river bank the best they can. If the flatboat came down the Ohio, the crew follows the Natchez Trace. That's a trail through the woods from Natchez all the way to Nashville, Tennessee. Often there are robbers along the trail—that's bad for the boatmen."

"Don't think I ever want to sign on for flatboat crew!" Abe said. He watched a small keelboat headed upstream, moving very slowly as the crew labored with poles to push her against the current. After a long sigh, he added, "Not sure I'll ever sign on again for a keelboat either, Barney. Coming back up the old Mississippi would be so slow and such hard work!"

Barney gave him a quick glance, but there was no more talk while they signaled to Captain Byrne to pull left to dodge a planter.

After many bends in the river, close calls in dodging planters and sawyers, and avoiding sandbars, they passed Little Prairie, which had only a few scattered cabins. A few miles farther, they pulled up for the night alongside one of the many wooded islands. The *Rosalie* was tied, fore and aft, to a pair of sturdy trees at the foot of a gently sloping bank.

Abe was tired and slept better that night—until about two o'clock in the morning. He awoke very suddenly, for there

123

was a terrible sound, a great roar that seemed to surround the whole boat. He grabbed the side board of the bunk to keep from falling to the floor.

Barney, clad in his long underwear, was standing in the aisle, his thin red hair standing on end. Captain Byrne, pulling on his trousers, came out of his cabin. As the *Rosalie* shuddered and rocked violently, the captain reached up a hand to help Abe down to the floor.

Mr. Lagrande, with Antoinette clinging to him, opened the curtain. "What in heaven's name was that?" he asked.

"Don't know—but best we all get into warm clothes," Captain Byrne said.

They scarcely had time to do that before great trouble came. Suddenly the boat rocked until it seemed about to turn over. As the mooring lines creaked with the extra pull on them, the sound was nearly lost in loud shrieking from outside and the frightened cries of the crew. The boat righted herself with an enormous splash and bounce.

The men who slept on the deck were all on their feet, holding onto anything attached to the boat. "Captain! We'll all be killed!" Mike's voice rose in terror, and the other men were all talking at once. There came the unmistakable sound of great trees breaking and crashing to the ground.

"Hold on, all of you!" Captain Byrne commanded. "I'll be out in a moment and we'll check."

"Stay here with Mr. Lagrande, Abe," he added. "Come on, Barney. Let's see what's going on." He lighted the lantern that hung from his cabin ceiling, while Barney hastily pulled on his boots and warm jacket. The two men went out to the foredeck.

124

A moment later, the captain's voice had a strange, strained sound as he cried out, "Oh, God help us!"

CHAPTER 10

The River's Gone Wild!

"The river's gone wild!" Captain Byrne shouted. "Waves like on the ocean!" The next second there was another great shudder of the boat. Water washed over the deck and the *Rosalie's* cargo on the stern crashed and banged about. As a pause came the captain called out, "Hold on, everyone! Just hold tight and maybe it will quiet down."

Mr. Lagrande, with Abe and Toni, stood in the cabin doorway. Too confused at what was happening to speak English, he asked *"Capitaine, qu'est-ce qu'il y a?"*

Captain Byrne understood enough to know that Lagrande had less idea than he did as to what was going on. "It might be an earthquake, Mr. Lagrande. Never heard of one in these parts, but nothing else could make the river so wild!"

There was a moment of quiet in which Mr. Lagrande said, "Earthquake?" He turned to Toni. *"Un tremblement du terre,"* he said to her. Then he added, still speaking in French, "Stay close to Abe, my dear. I do not want to lose you, and I may be needed in some way by the captain." He squeezed her hand and then said to Abe, "Please keep hold of her hand while I get dressed so that I can be of help."

Just as Lagrande reached his cabin, another frightening sound began, a great rumbling deep down in the earth.

Barney, making his way in the blackness to check the boat's rear deck, shouted, "Hold on, everyone! The tree mooring the stern is falling!"

Then came an ear-splitting, screeching sound as the tree's great rootball was ripped from the earth, and the tree fell toward the keelboat.

"Brace yourselves!!" Captain Byrne shouted above the sound of splitting timber. The roar grew even louder, almost drowning out the tremendous splash as the tree hit the rear deck.

The boat shuddered and seemed about to tip over. The stern mooring line pulled taut, then suddenly broke, letting the stern swing wildly. On the fourth swing it came to a stop, held by the upper limbs of the tree. Barney, making his way along the running board on the side toward the bank, saw that branches covered the stern deck.

"Let it be for now," he told Captain Byrne as he came back to the foredeck. "She can't swing about while the tree is holding her."

Abe stood braced against the cabin door frame. He could feel Toni's small body trembling as he held her close. His own heart was pounding wildly. *What is happening? Will the boat break into pieces? The river is so wild—will we all be thrown into it? How can we escape?* He heard the crashing sound of another tree falling back on the island, the wild screams of night birds, and the terrible roar in the earth.

Toni suddenly shuddered and looked back toward her father as he left the cabin. "Steady, Toni," Abe said. "Hold onto me and don't let go, like your papa said. Maybe that was the worst of it—and the boat still seems all right."

There was a moment of sudden stillness and in that instant Abe saw and heard his mother again, as he had seen and heard her in the dream—*Oh, Abraham—I knew something bad would happen! Look out, look out!*

Abe shook his head to bring himself back to the present. His arm tightened around Toni as he looked into her fear-filled eyes. He was so afraid himself that there was nothing he could say to help her. The river had gone wild!

Then the moment of quiet ended and the roaring and screeching began again, louder than before.

The boat rocked, rising and then suddenly falling on the wild waves. The crash of cargo shifting and banging together in the hold and on the stern added to the strangeness of the outer world. Abe and Toni moved aside a bit to let Captain Byrne get by to go to his cabin for another lantern, and a minute or two later to let him and Mr. Lagrande out onto the deck.

George's voice rose above the screeching of wildlife. "We're all going to die!" he wailed over and over again. Abe saw that two men were down on their knees praying and the others were in a huddle, clinging together to keep from falling.

Captain Byrne called out, "Pull yourselves together, men! Let's see what we can do and not just bawl about what's happening. George, quit that yowling and come with me. Lagrande and I are going ashore to see if it would be better for all of us to leave the boat until this is over."

George seemed frozen with fear, and the captain grabbed his arm and shook him into attention. "Come on now. Help me with this gangplank. Let's see if we can get it to reach to the shore. You, Patrick—give George a hand. The rest of you, man the poles and try to keep us from swinging about so badly."

With help from Patrick, George got the gangplank in place, but it dropped quite steeply before it reached solid ground. Apparently the bank had caved in. When the captain had the lantern lighted, he and Barney and Mr. Lagrande carefully made their way ashore.

As he left the boat, Captain Byrne called back, "Mike, you're in charge while I'm off the boat. Get Paul and Charles to dump the warm ashes from the cooking fire into the river. We don't want the boat to catch on fire on top of all that's already happened."

"Aye, sir," Mike answered, and a moment later, with a great sizzling sound, the ashes in the sheet metal box were dumped overboard. The sound had hardly died when Patrick cried out, "Oh, me sainted mother help us! The island's falling apart!"

He was right. Great chunks of the earth were breaking away, sliding into the river. The boat's prow swung away from the bank, straining at the remaining mooring line. Mike saw that the gangplank was about to slide off the deck, its far end no longer on solid ground. He grabbed it just in time to keep from losing it in the blackness of the river. He and Charles managed to pull it onto the deck. The river seemed a little less in upheaval. Was it all over?

The flickering light of the lanterns had disappeared. No one spoke; each person peered anxiously into the blackness of the night and heard the strange sounds all about—yowls of bobcats, shrieks of frantic wild fowl, groans of ancient trees resisting the pulling of their roots from the earth. At last the lantern light of the men on shore came closer.

The captain's sturdy figure could just be seen when suddenly there was another shock, not nearly as violent as the first one, but enough for some of the men to lose their balance.

"Hold on, men!" Mike ordered. "Gonna need you to help get them back on board. Get on your feet and stand to the poles! Push us close to the bank so Cap'n can board!" All followed the order except Charles, who was on his knees praying. Mike yelled, "You, Charles! Get off your knees and help me get them on board! Give me a hand with this gangplank!"

"O, mon Dieu!" Charles moaned. "Save us, save us!" he cried out in French. Mike's second shout, "CHARLES!" brought him to his feet. A moment later, Charles and Mike were extending hands to the three men to help them climb the unsteady plank.

"You first," Captain Byrne said, and pushed Mr. Lagrande toward the outstretched hands.

Abe, in the cabin doorway, held Toni's hand firmly. She was crying out in French, "Oh, Papa! Do not fall, Papa! *Ne tombes pas, Papa!"* as her father's feet slipped on the bank, which seemed to have sunk about two feet lower than it had been when the boat was tied. Mr. Lagrande reached out, and Mike and Charles pulled him up and onto the deck.

130

Abe couldn't keep Toni from rushing over to throw her arms around him.

A moment later, Captain Byrne and Barney were also back on board, and the gangplank was pulled onto the deck. Barney hung one of the lanterns over the cabin doorway on its hook, and in its flickering, swaying light, Abe saw that the captain's usually ruddy face was pale.

"What did you see, Cap'n?" Mike asked. "Should we all go on shore?"

Captain Byrne shook his head. "No, no!" He glanced at Barney. "We almost lost Barney. He was leading the way and we came to the biggest split in the earth you ever saw! It was three or four feet across! And the lantern light didn't show the bottom or the end in either direction. No, we'll not budge from the boat until dawn—if dawn ever comes after this terrible night!"

The men stood about, mouths agape and eyes wide. Suddenly there was a loud rumble, seeming to come from the north, down in the earth itself. As it surrounded the boat, the *Rosalie* gave a great shudder. "Drop to the deck, everyone! Hold on!"

This was the first of many aftershocks sending the boat to rocking and tilting so that it was in danger of overturning at any moment. Through it all, terror-stricken birds and animals shrieked, trees snapped and the deafening roar of the river joined with the frightening rumble from down in the earth. The *Rosalie's* joints creaked so that the men wondered if she could possibly hold together.

It seemed quieter after a while, and some of the crew stretched out on the deck to rest. The Lagrandes went back

131

to their quarters and Abe put his blanket on the floor beneath his bunk. Captain Byrne stayed on the deck with the crew, but he could not sleep. At the first faint streaks of dawn—copper-colored on that unforgettable December 16, 1811—the captain heard a new sound above the men's snores, something bumping against the boat's sides.

Peering into the murky half-light, he saw a skiff go by with a man lying face down in it. As the skiff slid past, the captain heard a faint call for help, but a great mass of logs followed right after the boat. There was no way the poor soul could be helped. The continuing bumping and scraping made Captain Byrne wonder how long the *Rosalie* could hold together. In the dim morning light he saw great foamy waves traveling down the river carrying heaps of driftwood, logs and even whole trees.

Barney was awakened by the bumping sounds, and some of the other men moved restlessly in their sleep. Barney was standing at the captain's side when another shock hit and brought everyone awake and back to the reality of the earthquake. The *Rosalie* shuddered violently and the mooring line at the prow, the only rope that held them from going downriver, screeched as if it must surely break.

"Barney, we've got to get another line. If that one snaps we'll be helpless!" Captain Byrne called out. He made his way through the men to the coil of rope. "Give us a hand, Mike," he added, and Mike got to his feet.

Barney could barely make out shapes as he peered down at the river bank. He said, "I can make it ashore with the line, Cap'n. But I swear, either the river has riz, or the bank dropped down!" He paused, and then, with a great leap, shouted, "Here I go!"

Mike cried out as he saw Barney slip on the muddy bank. But the brawny mate clawed at a young tree trunk and pulled himself up. "Toss me the line!" he yelled, and Mike sent it hurtling across the gap just as a bleary-eyed Abe came out to the deck.

He joined the men, all on their feet now, watching as Barney caught the line. He slipped and slid up the sloping bank to find a new mooring tree.

"Don't go too far, Barney!" the captain yelled. "Remember that big ditch. We don't want to lose you in it." Barney's reply was lost against the loud outcry of a bobcat and a pair of screech owls, and the rumbling in the earth. In a few minutes, he had chosen a tree that seemed to be holding to the earth, secured the rope and was ready to board the boat. Some of the men had the gangplank out for him. They gripped it tightly. With one leap he was on it and then on board.

Except for the strange cries from the wildlife, a calm seemed to settle over the river. Captain Byrne said, "We'll stay where we are until we can see well enough to judge what we should do. Get some more rest while you can, men."

Most of the men stretched out once more to rest, too tired to remain awake in spite of the strange noises and the heaving and rocking of the boat. One by one, they began to snore.

Mr. Lagrande and Toni had come out to see what was happening, but they went back into the men's cabin. Toni did not want to be alone in the ladies' cabin and she and her father had blankets on the floor beside his bunk. Abe went back inside also. Lying on the floor alongside Barney's bunk, he could only roll about restlessly and worry. Was his family all right? The trouble seemed to be coming from the north—as far north as St. Louis? He hoped not.

Barney and Captain Byrne stayed on their feet in the doorway to the deck. They stood in silence, trying to see what was going on. Finally Captain Byrne, smothering a yawn, said, "You and I had better stretch out too, Barney, until it's light enough to see better." The two men lay down on the little space still left on the deck. Barney, exhausted, slept after only a few minutes.

Daylight never did really come that morning, but there was a coppery look that could have been sunrise when another sound wave, an underground rumbling, came toward the boat from upriver. Again the boat shook. Several of the men sat up. Barney jumped in his sleep and then opened his eyes.

"Terrible dream," he muttered, groggily.

"No dream could be worse than what we've been through, Barney." The captain stood peering into the murky light.

Barney shook his head as if to clear it. "Oh, my sainted mother! The earthquake—"

By this time, most of the men were raising themselves cautiously from the deck. Abe and the Lagrandes came to the cabin doorway.

"There've been more than twenty aftershocks so far," the captain said. He peered at his big pocket watch. "Looks like it's about seven o'clock. Seems forever since this started."

"What time did that first big one come?" Barney asked.

"Just a bit after two. Now," Captain Byrne went on, "watch your step if you go ashore. We don't know what else might have happened in the night, but we know that great crack is there. Paul and Abe, get a fire going on shore for a bit of breakfast. Likely we have a rough day ahead!"

Josh was first off the boat, jumping down onto the bank without waiting for the gangplank to be pushed out. A moment later he was sliding into the murky brown water. When he clambered back up, he looked like he'd rolled in mud.

"Don't any more of you jump," Barney ordered. They propped the gangplank against a large rock that apparently had been uncovered in the upheaval of the earthquake, for no one remembered seeing it the evening before. Mr. Lagrande held Toni's hand tightly as they made their way down the gangplank, following the captain.

As her father helped Toni across the mud, a horrifying cry of a wild fowl came from close above them. Toni threw her arms about her father, and Abe heard her cry out, "Oh, Papa! *Nous allons perir!*" Abe heard Mr. Lagrande say soothingly, *"Non, nous n'allons pas perir, ma cherie,* we are not going to die! The earthquake will not wreck the boat." He held her until she became more calm.

Abe thought, *I know how she must feel—I'm scared, too!*

Mr. Lagrande found a fallen tree beyond the area where the breakfast fire would be built. "We shall sit on this tree trunk, Antoinette. Soon we will be away from all this."

When he and Paul had a fire burning, Abe went back on board to find the cornmeal sack. While he was on the deck, he glanced to the east. The sun, still low in the smoky sky, was a strange, copper-colored ball of fire. The air was heavy, thick and smelled of sulphur.

Abe's thoughts turned to his mother's words. Had the strange weather of the whole year been a sign that this terrible earthquake was coming? Was that comet traveling across the night sky a warning of what was about to happen? *If Mama hears about this she'll be awfully worried about me. I wish I could let her know that I'm all right.*

The men came back from their survey of the island. Disbelief was etched on their faces. Captain Byrne said, "Not very far back we came to that ditch we saw last night. It is a very dangerous split in the ground. Anyone who gets too close might never get out."

"Could you see the end, now that daylight is here?" Mr. Lagrande asked.

"No. It looked to me like it might go nearly to the end of the island. The sooner we can get on down the river, the better. From the direction of those roaring sounds, I would guess that the heart of this quake is a little north and west of us, maybe up around New Madrid. Things might get better as we get farther south."

Barney was shaking his head. "You wouldn't believe it! Dead fish lying a long way from the riverbank, like a giant tossed them ashore! Dead chipmunks and birds, too.

And trees down everywhere! If we'd been tied under a bluff, we'd probably all have been killed."

Captain Byrne said, "Seems to me we chose well to tie to a sloping bank. Looks like that low bluff over on the riverbank has fallen half away. Could have buried us in mud."

When the men had all been fed, the captain ordered, "Put out the fire, Abe. Men, take the food you have left and get back aboard. I have a feeling that more is coming. Hear that rumble in the earth?"

The men heard it, and didn't need to be told again to board the boat, immediately after Mr. Lagrande and Toni. Paul took the cooking implements on board as Abe scooped up soil to smother the fire. Then he hurried toward the gangplank. Suddenly he lost his balance and fell to the ground.

"Hey! The ground is rolling!" he yelled as he got to his knees and then tried to stand.

"Come on, Matey! Grab my hand!" Barney had come back to reach out to the boy. The boat was riding up and down on great waves, even though she was still tied to the mooring tree. Abe lunged and staggered, but managed to get onto the plank and was pulled on board by his big friend.

Lightning flashed in the murky sky, and the earth rumbles became louder. There was the crash of another tree falling.

"Let's get on the way," Captain Byrne said. "I'm not at all sure we might not be swallowed up into the earth, along with this whole island. We'll get as far down the river as we can while it is daylight. Barney and Mike—

loose the bow lines. Josh and Patrick, get to the stern and get us free of the fallen tree."

The orders were quickly followed. With Barney and Mike back on board, and the gangplank pulled in, Captain Byrne shouted, "Shove off, men!"

With their poles and oars and a great deal of labor, the boatmen pushed the *Rosalie* free of the tree's hold. As Captain Byrne and Barney went up to the roof, Barney said, "Cap'n, 'tain't my place to be givin' orders to you, but hold onto that rudder pole so we don't lose you in this wild river!"

Abe was starting up the ladder too, but Barney called out, "Stay down there, Matey! Your job now is to look after the passengers."

The moment the *Rosalie's* prow swung out into the current, they were pulled almost sideways. "Ain't nothin' right on this old river this mornin'," Barney muttered. "Shoreline ain't like it used to be. And I'd swear there's a heavin' goin' on, over on the land, like the ground was ocean waves! It'll be a miracle if we don't get busted up on a snag. No way we can miss 'em!"

Every man was busy with a pole, trying to clear the way for the keelboat. The entire river seemed one great raft of floating logs, any one of which could cause a break in the hull.

They were hardly started when the great roar came again. But this time it was more terrifying than before, for suddenly the river seemed to form a great wave in the middle and then to drop away so much that the river bottom could be seen. The *Rosalie* was lifted into the air, and when she came down she was moving back upstream.

"The river's going backward!" Barney yelled. "Hold on—hold on tight!" Losing his footing, Barney dropped to the cabin roof. Looking back, he saw that Captain Byrne was also down, and the rudder pole was waving in the air.

With a monstrous heaving, a great groaning, and a jumping about of barrels and boxes of cargo, the next minutes seemed a lifetime. The boat was back alongside the island where they'd spent the night. And then, suddenly, all was very quiet.

"Save me! Save me!" came a cry from the river.

CHAPTER 11

Abe and Gus in Trouble

"Cap'n, someone's adrift on a log! He's grabbin' hold of our skiff!" George, back at the stern to put overturned barrels back in place, had glanced down at the troubled water before returning to his poling position. "He's tryin' to climb aboard!"

Captain Byrne called out, "Let him be! Back to your post, George!" Then he muttered, "It's just a wonder we still have our skiff, but we don't need any more people on board."

George turned away from the sight of the unknown person clinging to the skiff. As he was stooping to pick up his pole and return to his work position, the strange quiet and exposed patches of riverbed suddenly ended. The wind roared. The keelboat lurched forward as water rushed over the uncovered river bottom, returning the flow to its normal downriver direction. The rumbling of the earth and the howls and shrieks from the woods began once more.

"Yikes!" yelled George, as his feet flew out from under him. The sudden freeing of the *Rosalie* sent the crew sprawling along the running boards. The men fell like dominoes in a row, and their curses filled the air. Abe fell on the foredeck.

Barney too, lost his balance on the roof. Looking back, he saw that the captain had also fallen. He called, "You all right, Cap'n?"

"Will be as soon as this cantankerous river settles down. Looks like we're heading downriver again."

And they were, with a great rush. There was no time to think about the fellow clinging to the skiff. It took every man's attention to keep the boat from crashing into the stream of logs, whole trees, broken boards from boats, and even a section of wall from a log cabin swept along in the wild river.

As the *Rosalie* swung on with the rapid current, there came again the plaintive scream from just beyond the stern, "Save me! Help! Someone help me!"

After a moment, the captain called, "ABE! "

Abe quickly climbed the ladder high enough to see the captain. "Yes, sir! Want me to come up there?"

Captain Byrne shouted, "NO! Get back to the stern where you can reach the skiff line. There's a fellow in the water down there."

Abe made his way past the men laboring with their poles. When he got to the stern deck, he looked down at the skiff. Yes, there was someone down there clinging to the skiff rail with his hands while his knees were pressed tightly to a log on which he rode. Abe turned to look up toward the captain in his usual place handling the rudder.

"Yes, sir—I'm back here, Cap'n. Should I help him get into the skiff?"

Captain Byrne took his attention from handling the rudder for a quick downward glance. "That fellow looks kind of familiar...oh, lordy, I hope it's not who I think it is! We've had enough bad luck to last the rest of the trip."

Abe was peering down at the skiff—someone looking more like an overgrown drowned rat than a human being was clinging to the small boat. And then Abe saw who it was. He turned away and called up to Captain Byrne, "Yeah, Cap'n—you're right. It's old Gus, half drowned. Should I help him on board?"

The captain, busy controlling his rudder pole, didn't look down as he answered, "Gus—just what we need—that lazy good-for-nothin'. Do what you think best, Abe. I can't be bothered with that no-good."

To his own surprise, Abe found himself feeling sorry for Gus. *Can't just let him drown—that would be wrong and I'd hate myself.* Gazing down at Gus, the lines Colonel Easton had him memorize came to Abe. *To thine own self be true. Thou canst not then be false to any man.*

Abe leaned over to reach the iron ring to which the line that held the skiff in tow was attached. He saw that the rope was already frayed, and wouldn't hold much longer. Grabbing the line beyond the frayed area, he pulled the skiff closer so that it touched the end of the keel, a big wooden beam. "Got to re-knot this line before we lose our skiff—soon as I pull Gus in," he muttered.

Carefully, he climbed out of the *Rosalie,* and letting go of the line, lowered himself into the small boat. He almost lost his balance and dropped to his knees as the skiff lurched suddenly. Feeling the cold water in the boat bottom swirl over his boots and pants, he knew he had to act quickly. Gus, his legs still clutching the log, moved along with the boat and looked up hopefully. Abe took a deep breath and then said as pleasantly as he could muster, "Well, if it isn't my old friend Gus!"

142

When Gus replied, his voice had lost all its arrogance. It was pitiful and pleading. "I—I can't hang on much longer, Abe. Help me—please take me on your boat—or I'll just die here..." The voice faded on those words as if Gus were about to die then.

Abe waited a moment to catch his breath and calm himself. Then he said, "Yeah, Gus. I should let you drown, but I can't even do that to a scroungy pup. So I guess I'll have to help you." He moved along on his knees until he was alongside Gus, who still clung to his log and the skiff side rail.

Abe could reach to Gus' shoulders, but he couldn't see any way to lift him into the skiff. "You gotta help, too, Gus. I can't lift you outta the river. Come on now—let go the log and raise up so I can get my hands under your arms."

Gus' head came up, his mouth hung open, but he made no move to help himself. "Help me, Abe—" came in a voice nothing like Gus' usual sneering way of speaking to Abe. "I almost got killed—" he whined. "I can't hang on any longer."

"Yeah, Gus—do what I say. I'll help you. Come on now, before another bump comes—get your feet onto that log you're sittin' on, so I can get a hold on you. You gotta do that or I can't get a grip on you to help you into the skiff. Come on, pull yourself up!"

Gus made an effort to raise his body. Slowly he got his feet onto the log and could crouch over the skiff as Abe gripped his arms. His shirt and pants and even his winter underwear were ripped and hanging in tatters. Abe saw

143

that he was badly bruised. In a gentler voice, he said, "All right, Gus. Here we go!"

Abe fell back in the tremendous effort of dragging Gus from the water and into the boat. His back struck against the wooden seat board, and Gus came toppling face down on top of him, his big feet, bare and with leaves and twigs sticking to them, hung out over the water.

Abe felt pain all through his body. For a moment he lay there, weighed down by the bigger boy's body, the edge of the seat board cutting into his back. With all his might he pushed himself up and rolled Gus over into the skiff.

And then the keelboat swerved, suddenly swinging away from a tree that had fallen out into the channel as the bank gave way. The tow line snapped taut and the skiff swung about, out of control. At almost the same moment there was another jolting earthquake aftershock. Gus, his voice returned, screamed, "Whatcha tryin' to do to me? Oh, my back, my back—it's broke!"

But Abe didn't answer. The jolt had thrown him down again, knocking the breath from his lungs as he fell backwards, this time with his rib cage against the seat board. For a moment he wondered if he'd ever breathe again.

He lay with his eyes closed, trying to get his strength back, wishing himself safely back on board the *Rosalie*— and Gus far, far away.

Gus moaned again. "Help me, Abe."

Abe muttered, "Help yourself, you big lout." And then he shook his head, pulled himself forward and sat up. He saw how battered Gus looked and how he was shivering from head to foot. He felt a bit ashamed of his mean

144

thoughts—he'd have to get the two of them on board the *Rosalie*—and fast.

He turned around to pull the skiff in closer to the keelboat. But the line lay dangling in the water, snapped by the strain of the aftershock. The skiff was adrift, stuck against a mass of tree limbs. Where was the *Rosalie?*

The force of another wave pushed the small boat farther into the brushy tree top that trapped it. The leaves of the past summer were gone, but a tangle of twigs scratched Abe's face. He tried to push them away and free his head and shoulders, grasping a sturdier limb to keep from falling into the water. He peered downriver just in time to see the *Rosalie* rounding a bend.

"Oh, oh, ow-w-w! Help me get up, Abe."

"Help yourself. I've got enough to do." Abe looked about, sizing up the situation. "We're in a heap o' trouble, Gus. We gotta catch up with the *Rosalie,* somehow." He looked for the paddle that was kept in the bottom of the skiff. "Lucky for us. Here's the paddle." Abe did his best to guide the skiff's direction with the paddle, trying to keep it from getting tangled in some of the floating debris.

Gus just lay there in front of him, taking up most of the space in the small boat. Finally he said, mournfully, "What are we gonna eat? Ain't had nothin' since yesterday."

"Sorry. I didn't pack a picnic lunch for this boat ride." Abe couldn't keep the sarcasm from his voice. *Why did I get into this fix?*

"Won't they turn around and come lookin' for us?"

Gus's whine was almost more than Abe could stand. He tried his best to make his own voice civil as he answered. "They can't turn the boat around in this earthquake mess. Besides, they're so busy tryin' to keep from wreckin' the boat against all this floatin' stuff that likely they haven't even missed me yet."

He thought a minute, recalling that a dangerous passage lay a short way down the river from the island where they had spent that awful night. *What was it called?* A fleeting thought of Toni came to mind as he remembered. *Devil's Race Ground, that was it.* It was a bad place even without an earthquake, a narrow channel with snags, rocks and fast running water. They'd never be able to get the *Rosalie* back through it, even if they tried. No, he'd simply have to try to take the skiff down the river until they caught up with the keelboat when it made an overnight stop.

At last Gus was pulling himself into a sitting position, facing forward in the skiff. Abe, behind him on the seat, turned around and pushed with the paddle to make the boat run closer to the left, toward the lower end of the long island. "We're goin' back over to the island, if I can make this boat turn the right way. Captain and Barney saw dead fish thrown onto the land from the river when they went lookin' this morning—better 'n no food at all."

"Ugh—dead fish! How'd we cook 'em?"

"Well, while we're headin' over to the island, maybe you can catch one that's still alive. Would fresh fish please your majesty?" Abe reached into his coat pocket and smiled at what he found there. "My light bottle! It's what I use to get a fire started when I help Paul with the cookin'. Got a little bundle of splints for it, too, and my knife.

We're in luck—if we can find some dry leaves and twigs I can get a fire started." He thought a moment longer, and then added, "People always need water, but there's lots of that around. We won't die of thirst, for sure. Let's get goin'."

Abe planned to maneuver the skiff out of the tree limbs and somehow head it back over to the island. If he got some food into Gus, maybe Gus could help manage the skiff as they moved toward Devil's Race Ground. It would be a two-man job. He could make poles by trimming a couple of pieces of driftwood with his knife.

Abe pushed at the larger limbs, working the skiff away from the tree. Gus continued to moan and complain.

"You're sure not any help, Gus. You could at least shut up for a while. If you don't, I might even knock you out with this paddle!" He sat still for a moment, waving the paddle threateningly.

Gus raised his arm to shield his head, and said, "All right, Abe. But I really do hurt somep'n awful."

"Yeah," Abe said. "I s'pose you do, but you'll have to just put up with it. How come you didn't stay on the flatboat?"

A look of horror came into Gus' eyes. "Ain't no flatboat no more. She broke apart last night. The other fellows was ridin' on a big part, like a raft, but they wouldn't help me when I tried to climb on board. Then more of those horrible waves came and...logs banged against me, and...and the river jest grabbed me and threw me around until I hung onto that log..." A great sob shook Gus, and to Abe's horror, he broke down and cried.

"Sorry, Gus," Abe muttered and concentrated on directing the skiff to the island. Its shore near the southern end was only about thirty feet away. Abe was grateful when he heard the sound of the skiff's bottom scraping a rock. He jumped out and pulled the boat as far as he could onto the bank, and tied the remainder of the tow rope to a tree.

"Out you come," he said and reached in to help Gus onto land. Gus meekly climbed out.

"Now. Gus, you keep the skiff from being pulled away while I look for something to eat," Abe ordered. He began to walk and a second later lost his balance. "Hey, the ground is rollin' like the water! Need sea legs to even walk!"

He struggled a few feet up the bank and saw a real treasure. "Gus, I found a sack of cornmeal from someone's boat!" The wave of the earth passed as he stood for a moment before lifting the sack. He found it heavy with water, undoubtedly washed away from one of the wrecked flatboats or skiffs that had come down on the wild waters. The cloth had burst and much of the meal had been lost, but there was enough to hold off starvation.

"Won't need those dead fish, Gus. I'll flatten out lumps of this and bake them—delicious corncakes for your majesty."

Gus was sitting on the bank, holding onto the tow rope. He smiled wanly at Abe's attempt at humor as Abe, walking carefully, put the sack into the boat and turned toward the trees. "I'm looking for dead leaves and things under the trees. There should be some dry enough to burn," he called back.

"I learned a lot from Paul," Abe said as he built a small fire on a flat rock. Then he shaped some of the wet cornmeal into flattened cakes and laid them on the rock alongside the fire. "These won't be fancy corncakes—likely the worst ones you ever ate, but maybe they'll give you enough strength so you can help me get the skiff down to the *Rosalie*. You stay here and tend the skiff and keep the fire going while I go look for a limb you can use for a pole. When I get back, the rock should be hot enough to bake the corncakes."

Meekly, Gus nodded as Abe walked into the woods. Abe walked with his legs far apart to keep his balance on the unsteady earth. He remembered the long, deep trench the earthquake had caused, and watched for it. He soon saw a limb that could be used as a pole, even though it was bent a bit. As he stooped to pick it up, he pushed a bush aside. Just in time, he saw that one more step and he'd be tumbling into the river. The land ended! Peering downward, he saw that a great chunk of what had been the island now lay several feet away in the river.

"End of my walk," he said aloud and turned back, carrying the pole. He followed a different route back, and along the way found two dead quail huddled together. He picked them up and tossed them into the skiff when he reached it. "May need to cook these tonight," he said to Gus.

A sad looking Gus was putting more twigs on the little fire. Abe partially cleared a bit of the heated rock and moved the two flattened cornmeal lumps closer to the flames.

"Got you a pole to work with," Abe said. He picked up the pole and broke away a small branch growing from it, peeling off a long strip of bark as he did so. Gus said nothing as Abe put the pole into the skiff. "You can peel off more of the bark later. I'll let you use my knife if you won't let it fall into the river." As Abe spoke, he took the knife from the sheath that hung from his belt and used it to turn over the two thin corncakes.

A few minutes later, he scraped the corncakes loose and handed them to Gus, who eyed them distastefully. He bit off half of one and chewed it a long time before he could swallow.

"Pretty tough, aren't they?" Abe said as he watched.

"Awful—and they taste like the river."

Nevertheless, Gus made his way through the two thin corncakes. He had just swallowed the last bite when a deep rumble in the earth sounded again. It came from the north. Then, from the same direction, came the distressed cry of wild birds.

"Come on, Gus. That means more trouble. We'd best get going while we can! Help me get the boat afloat."

For once, Gus had no complaint. The two of them got the skiff into the water and pushed clear of the island. They both got in and Abe turned the paddle in the water, using it as a rudder to head the boat downstream. Within seconds, it began to rock violently, dipping down at the bow and then rising.

"Get down on your knees and hold on!" Abe ordered, and he, too, was on his knees on top of the precious paddle. "Here she comes!" A huge wave lifted the small craft, tossing her several feet into the air. She landed with a force that made both boys cry out. For the next minutes, the current swept her along without aid from the paddle or the new pole. Both boys had all they could do to stay with the skiff until this newest tremor ended.

"That was an easy one, compared to a couple we had this morning," Abe said. But when they could sit up and see what was ahead, they had to get into action quickly to round a bend. Gus moaned loudly as he took hold of the rough pole, but he did his best to work with it. They made it safely around the bend, and were swept along for a fast trip past several small islands.

They had just rounded two bad curves when they saw just ahead another curve, thick with whole trees washed into it, and held back by an old blockade of planters. "Must be Devil's Race Ground!" Abe cried out.

He peered ahead as the little skiff was carried toward the barrier on the swift current. He turned the paddle-rudder as he shouted to Gus, "Pole her toward the right, Gus! I can see where the *Rosalie* broke through!"

Gus pushed the pole against the river bottom and the snags to help veer the boat away from a smash-up, as Abe worked frantically with the paddle. In a few seconds, they were held sideways against the brushy barrier.

Now the headlong rush was stopped, but the wild river pushed relentlessly against the side of the skiff as if to swallow it in the great mass of brush. The boat rocked dangerously, rising against the brush and then dropping down, nearly tipping the boys out into the swirling, foaming water.

Abe saw that they needed to go farther along the tree limbs and logs to get to the opening the *Rosalie* had made. "Gus, we can bushwhack our way to the opening."

"Don't know as I can—" Gus had put his pole in the boat bottom and grabbed the side rail of the skiff to keep from falling out. "If I let go I'll fall into the river."

Abe had almost fallen himself. "We'll do it kneeling. You've got to let go of the rail or we'll be here rocking in this mess all night! And this is no cradle—we'll be buried by another big old tree comin' down on top of us. Come on now. When I count to three we'll both grab the brush and pull!"

Carefully, Gus straightened up and as Abe yelled "Three!" quickly reached for a handhold in the brush. The two worked together, managing to get the skiff a few inches closer to the break-through with each pull on the brush.

At last they were on their way through, finding a narrow channel of open water where the brush had not yet come together after the passage of the *Rosalie*. The rushing water carried the little boat through without help from the boat's passengers.

"We made it through!" Abe shouted as the boat slid downward over a little waterfall. "The devil didn't get us, Gus!"

Bracing himself with the paddle, he stood up to see what was ahead. There was an island just a few yards away and to the left, and then another sharp bend in the river. "Time to paddle and pole so we'll catch up with the *Rosalie* before dark," he called to Gus.

He lifted the paddle and stood up to put it into the water. And then it happened. The boat lurched as a little whirlpool caught the bow.

"Oh, OH!" Abe yelled as he toppled over into the brush-filled stream, the paddle dropping from his hands as he fell. His head struck a log, and he went down into the darkness.

CHAPTER 12

The Rosalie, at Last!

Abe could see only dark, murky water and a network of tree branches that blocked his way. Needing air, he struggled to find a way through the underwater thicket and rise to the surface. His head again hit the large log, this time on its underwater side. Frantic for air, he struggled to move clear of it. He could not hold his breath much longer—

Thrashing with his arms, trying to swim away from the log, he tried once again to push upward. This time he rose just high enough to gasp for breath, but he was trapped in a tangle of tree limbs that pulled him down again. He felt them on his face, scratching his nose, his eyelids. Treading water, he tried to move his face clear of the prickly branches so that he could see.

"Carson! Where are you?"

Abe heard Gus calling him, but he couldn't answer. His head was under water again, as he was pulled down by the river current and branches of the sawyer in which he was caught. He clawed at the twigs until he grasped a limb sturdy enough to help him to the surface and get his head out of the water.

"Here—" he gasped, and coughed out water, trying to get air into his lungs.

154

Gus, safe in the skiff, was wielding the paddle. He called, "Hold onto that big log. I'm trying to pull the skiff close as it'll go!"

Grasping a sturdy limb to keep from going under the mass of driftwood again, Abe opened his eyes and rubbed the water from them with his free hand. He let go of the tree limb and pushed toward the log, but the tangle of limbs grabbed at his clothing.

"Reach the pole out to me, Gus!"

Gus did as he asked, kneeling in the skiff to keep from joining Abe in the wildly circling water. Abe reached out and grasped the pole with both hands. Gus pulled as Abe pushed with his legs and feet against the tree that had trapped him.

"Hold your end tight, Gus!" Abe went along the pole hand over hand until he could reach the skiff. After another minute of struggle, he was climbing into the boat as Gus helped him out of the water.

It was none too soon. Abe had scarcely got to a sitting position when the earth was shaking again and the skiff went scooting along with the current. Abe and Gus could only hold onto the boat rails, hoping the boat would not be overturned by the branches that seemed to be trying to entrap it. Then at last there was more open water and the boat was once more floating instead of bouncing. As the mild tremor ended, Abe, dripping wet, began to shiver and his teeth chattered in the December air.

"G-g-gus—I th-th-think we'd better head for that island just ahead, unless you can see the *Rosalie.*"

Gus peered ahead. "Cain't see no boat at all," he said. He picked up the paddle and handed it to Abe as he took up the pole. "Lucky for you, Abe—I pulled the paddle into the boat. You dropped it when you started to fall, you know. Could have been lost if I hadn't saved it."

Even now, Gus has to brag! Abe thought, but smiled a bit and said, "Th-thanks," through his chattering teeth.

They maneuvered the boat into the foaming, driftwood filled water, trying to reach the sloping bank of an island. They pulled in between two trees that had fallen into the water, their root masses still partially held in the disturbed ground. When the skiff was secured to tree limbs, both boys waded ashore. Abe plunged his right hand into his coat pocket and grinned as he pulled out the water-proof bag with his fire-lighting equipment. "Sure glad this didn't get lost in the river!"

Still shivering in his cold, wet clothing, Abe hunted about for dry grass, twigs and leaves to start a fire while Gus picked up some of the broken tree limbs. As the fire built up, both boys came close to it to feel its warmth. Abe took off his boots and dumped out the water. Both boys stripped to their long-legged winter underwear and spread their wet clothing out to dry as much as possible. Teeth chattering, they huddled by the fire, feeding it with the driest wood they could find. After about an hour, darkness came. Still shivering with the cold, they dressed again, even though their clothing was still very damp.

"Gotta keep this fire fed all night," Abe said. "Likely there's bobcats and maybe worse on this island. Come on, Gus, let's build up our firewood pile." For once Gus joined in the task of gathering wood without complaining.

By the time they had enough wood stacked, they were glad to stay close to the light of the fire. The eerie sounds from both river and land added to their shivers even though the fire was warming them. All the creatures of nature, from the birds to the wolves, seemed to be wailing or howling with terror over what was happening to their homeland. Neither boy spoke of his deep down fears until there came another great heaving of the very ground on which they were sitting. Then they heard a mighty cracking, pulling sound of a huge tree tearing lose from its tortured roots.

"Watch out! Another tree is falling!" Abe yelled and both boys jumped to their feet. The great old tree fell with a tremendous crash some fifty feet from their little campsite, but its top branches reached out to where the skiff was tied.

"It's right where we were hunting for firewood a little while ago," Abe said. "We could have been killed!"

"Yeah—this is horrible. Abe, do you think we'll ever catch up with the *Rosalie?*"

Abe swallowed hard. "Sure hadn't planned on all this," he said. "But if we don't give up, we're sure to find the boat. Captain Byrne will be watching for us—probably worrying right now about what happened to us!"

Except for strange moaning sounds around them, it was quiet as they sat down again as close to the fire as possible. "I'm getting hungry," Abe said then and added, "Do you suppose those two little quail I found are still in the boat?"

Both boys got up. Abe plucked a burning piece of wood from the fire for a torch, and made his way to the skiff. He reached down into the prow. "We're in luck!" he called back to Gus. "We've got some supper!" He climbed into the skiff and reached for the two dead birds, now jammed up into the prow.

Each boy stripped the feathers from a bird, cleaned it in the river water and speared it onto a sharpened stick. They flattened some more of the unappetizing cornmeal to help stop the hunger pangs that each of them was feeling, and baked the small cakes on a hot stone.

As they roasted the birds over the fire, the night beyond their firelight settled into complete blackness. They were sitting side by side like old friends, when Abe said, "I sure thank you for helping me back into the boat, Gus. I was so tangled in that tree I could have drowned."

Gus said, "Yeah. Lucky for you I was there, wasn't it?"

"Yeah, sure was," Abe said and waited for Gus to remember why they were in this trouble, but Gus' mind didn't go in the direction of thanking Abe for his own rescue. Abe couldn't help but think, *I wouldn't have been in this fix if I hadn't rescued you, Gus!*

They sat in silence for a while. Abe heard Gus give a shivering sigh followed by a gulp. Gus took a deep breath and sighed. Finally he said, "I guess I should say thank you, too, Abe. I'd be dead now if you hadn't helped me get into the skiff."

Abe wondered if his thoughts had somehow got into Gus' mind. The loud screech of a wildcat made both boys inch a little closer to the fire. When they began to eat the half-done quail, Gus shuddered and said, "Some salt to put on this bird would make it taste better."

"That's for sure, Gus. But we'll catch up with the *Rosalie* and get some of Paul's cooking before we starve." Silence again. Then as he ate the last bit of meat from his quail, Abe remarked, "You and I aren't fighting, for the only time I can remember."

"Yeah. Guess you ain't so bad, after all."

Abe said nothing, but a little later, when Gus didn't offer to stay awake for first guard duty and had fallen asleep, he couldn't help but resent Gus' selfishness. He remembered hearing Colonel Easton saying once, "Misery acquaints a man with strange bedfellows." He'd told Abe that it was another of Shakespeare's wise sayings. *No one could have had more misery than me and Gus this day!*

Abe thought it was about two o'clock when he built up the fire and woke Gus. Gus looked half asleep as Abe stretched out, but Abe decided that even if Gus fell asleep, they'd be all right until morning. He was so tired he went to sleep immediately.

Abe's sleep didn't last long. It was still dark when he was awakened by the earth rolling and rumbling under them. Neither boy could stand up without falling. *Another aftershock!* Knowing that they'd be in serious trouble if the skiff was pulled loose, Abe decided they should put out the fire and get into the boat. They picked up their few belongings and climbed into the skiff, holding onto the rails. The little craft bounced so badly they were nearly thrown out, but it didn't tear loose from its moorings.

"That one was almost as bad as the first big one," Abe said.

"It couldn't have been as bad for you, shrimp," Gus said, going back into his old way of talking to Abe. "Your boat didn't break up under you like the flatboat did—" He paused, and then added, "You always had more friends, and you got all the breaks—" Abe realized that Gus was actually crying. He said nothing in reply.

Later, as they waited for dawn, Abe said, "Gus, you could make it better for yourself and people would like you, same as other guys. But you are always trying to blame other people for what happens to you." He paused a moment and then went on. "You've got to think more about the other guy. The only time I ever saw you helping someone else was when I was dumped in the river. And you always brag about how great you are. Nobody wants a friend like that."

Gus had no reply.

⌛ ⌛ ⌛

The first hint of daylight saw the two boys untying the skiff and heading down the Mississippi once more. They had been on the river about two hours when they sighted a bluff ahead on the left, with some kind of building on the top. As they drew closer, they saw a keelboat anchored below the bluff at the mouth of a small river.

"The *Rosalie!*" Abe shouted. With renewed energy they poled and paddled the skiff toward the boat that had almost become home to Abe. The building on the bluff could now be seen clearly, too, and it looked like some kind of log fort or blockhouse.

A group of people, men, women, and a few children, had gathered on the bluff to watch the arrival of the skiff.

Abe recognized some of the men from the *Rosalie*, including Captain Byrne. He was sure that he also saw Toni and her father. Toni's left hand was held by a woman Abe did not know, but as the skiff moved in toward shore Toni began to wave a greeting with her right hand, jumping up and down in joy. Abe waved back happily for just a moment before working to get the skiff beached.

Down on the riverbank, ready to moor the skiff and greet the arrivals, were Barney and Paul. "Ahoy, Matey!" Barney shouted. "Bring her in!"

Abe and Gus were soon climbing the bluff, made welcome not only by the people from the *Rosalie* but by the other people gathered there. The boys learned from Barney that these were earthquake victims who had lost their homes both up and down the river's shores. They had gathered at the old fort for shelter, and had been very welcoming to the crew of the *Rosalie*.

Captain Byrne came most of the way down the bluff to meet Abe. His eyes were a bit moist as he shook hands with the boy and then thrust an arm over Abe's shoulder, almost in a hug. "We've been worrying about you, Abraham. We were sure you'd catch up with us before night...but just the same, I didn't know if that old skiff would hold together."

Abe gulped, surprised to know that the captain really cared so much. After a moment he could say, "We tried to catch up with the *Rosalie* yesterday, Captain—but the earthquake kind of slowed us down. Sure was cold and dark on that island where we had to stop—and scary, too, with all the roaring and howling going on." Abe shuddered just thinking about it.

The captain said, in a tight voice, "Really missed you, lad!"

Abe felt toward Captain Byrne almost as he did toward his father. He was afraid he might start crying, but he took a big shivery breath because he must say something to this good man. But all he could get out was, "Thanks, Captain."

Gus was climbing the bluff with Barney and Paul as Abe went on with the captain, walking toward the blockhouse where there were more people, men women and children.

"All these people came here because they were so frightened by what was happening," the captain explained. "Some of them saw their cabins catch on fire, and some were terribly scared when their cabin moved with them inside and the ground all around was waving like a land ocean. It was all so terrible that they brought things they needed and came here to this sturdy blockhouse for safety. And it was a sight for sore eyes for us, too, with a cove for landing safely. This morning when you still were not here, we knew we had to find you before we went farther." He chuckled. "Barney would have hog-tied me to the mast if I'd ordered us to leave without you!"

They reached the top of the bluff. "Here's someone else who would have been very angry with me!" the captain added. Toni was still with her new friend, but she let go of the woman's hand to run to Abe. Mr. Lagrande was not far behind her.

"Oh, Abraham! I was so afraid—so afraid you were—" she was searching for a word—*"mort!"* She threw her arms around Abe and hugged him.

Mr. Lagrande said, over her head, "She was afraid you might have been killed, Abraham. We are all very glad to see you!"

Abe had never been happier, so happy that tears came to his eyes. He brushed them away in embarrassment and grinned widely.

Toni turned back after a moment to bring the woman she'd been standing with to meet Abe. "Madame Trudeau, this is my friend, Abraham Carson," Toni said. The lady held out her hand to Abe, and he shook it, feeling a bit awkward until he saw Madame Trudeau's warm smile. It made him feel at ease in just a moment.

"She can talk with me in French," Toni said, smiling up at her new friend. "I stayed in the fort with her and the other people all last night. We had such good fun!"

Soon afterward, Mr. Lagrande explained to Abe that Madame Trudeau had lost both her husband and her daughter of Toni's age in a fire that burned their cabin to the ground three months ago. She was as lonesome as Toni was, and the two had taken to each other immediately.

All this time, Gus had stood behind Abe and his welcoming friends. No one seemed inclined to greet him, just glancing at him and turning away. He trailed after Abe and Toni as the whole group walked toward the blockhouse.

When Toni welcomed Abe so heartily, Gus could stand it no longer. "Hello, Toni," he said loudly. "Ain't you gonna speak to me? My name's Gus."

Toni turned back to look at Gus. "How do you do, Gus?" she said, very politely. Then she immediately turned away.

"I saved Abe when he fell in the river," Gus volunteered. "Ain't you glad I was there to help him?"

Toni turned to Abe and said, "Oh, Abraham! Are you hurt?"

"I'm fine, Toni. Gus helped me get back into the boat."

Gus grinned. He said nothing about how Abe had first saved him from the river. Barney took Gus by the arm quite roughly and said, "If you'd shown up without Abe, I'd have tanned your worthless hide and held your head under the water 'til you drowned!"

Mr. Lagrande was near enough to hear the conversation. He stepped up to Gus, whose old pants were badly torn, and said, "I don't want you near my daughter in those torn clothes. You look indecent. Come down to the *Rosalie* with me. I have an extra pair of trousers and a shirt that will fit you, I'm sure." The two headed down the bluff.

Barney took Abe to one side when Madame Trudeau and Toni went into the blockhouse together. "Did you notice the sparkle in Miss Toni's eyes, Matey? It's partly 'cause you're back, but also 'cause she is so happy with this French lady. I don't like to think of how she'll feel when we leave here and she has to say goodbye."

"When will that be?" Abe asked.

"Cap'n wanted someone to go back upriver to look for you before we left if you didn't show up by noon. But we'd have had to borrow a boat from someone. We have quite a bit of work to do on the *Rosalie* before we start on down the river—but we should be ready to leave in the morning."

"That reminds me, I'm sure hungry for some good food!"

"Some of the men went off into the woods to hunt this morning—Mike and Josh and Patrick. They wanted to get some game to leave with these people who are in such great trouble. I expect they'll get enough to make some good meals for us, too."

One of the women came outside with a message for Captain Byrne. "We have been making a big pot of stew and some apple pudding, enough for everyone. We want you all to come for dinner."

"Thank you, ma'am. Don't have to ask us twice!" Captain Byrne said. "We'll be there as soon as all the men get back."

Soon afterward, the hunters returned with plenty of game for the keelboat crew, plus a good supply to leave with their hosts. George and Charles had been busy cutting a supply of firewood for the people, and were stacking it neatly near the blockhouse.

Gus had returned dressed better than Abe had ever seen him. Besides the trousers and a shirt Mr. Lagrande had given him, Captain Byrne had offered an old jacket and a pair of boots. "Not because he's worth it, but I don't like to see anyone shivering in the cold," the captain said.

Abe thought Gus looked taller in his fine clothes, holding his head up instead of slouching. He said, "Boy! You sure look dressed up! Come here a minute." He pretended to be pulling Gus' shirt straight, but he was whispering a reminder to Gus. "Thank the captain and Mr. Lagrande— they've been real good to you!"

Gus took the hint right away, thanking the captain and then Mr. Lagrande who had just joined the group. Gus said to him, "The clothes are real nice, Mr. Lagrande. Thank you."

Mr. Lagrande grunted a bit, like the captain, Abe thought. Then, looking right into Gus' eyes, Mr. Lagrande said, "It was worth it to have you respectably dressed in my daughter's company. Please try also to behave like a gentleman." He turned away abruptly and walked toward the blockhouse where Antoinette and Madame Trudeau were waiting for him.

The blockhouse was crowded with everyone inside to eat dinner, so the men of the group and the boatmen soon moved back outdoors, taking their plates with them and sitting on fallen tree trunks. Gus had wanted to eat with the women and children in the blockhouse, but Captain Byrne insisted that he and Abe go outside with the "menfolks."

As the blockhouse men finished dinner, they wanted to tell the visitors more about the earthquake and the loss of their frontier homes. "Terrible, terrible! Why are we being so greatly punished?" an old man asked, and every person seemed to have a horror tale to tell of how his house had fallen and burned or suddenly slid off its foundation rocks. They told of great cracks and holes in the earth, and the ground movement—"Like ocean waves," one man said.

Another man cut in, "I tell you, the river bottom was opened up! The water was gone, and then there was a wide crack in it, all along...you can see from this bluff. The next thing we saw was the water rushing back, and where the crack had been, a great water spout was shooting water as high as a treetop!"

"And the land just disappearing over there—never saw the likes of it!"

"The work of the devil!"

And so it went on, until one man, better dressed than most, took command. "I'll tell you why this happened," he said. "You've all seen the comet that's been in the sky every night for months until just a week or so ago. That there comet has two horns, and the earth rolled over one of them! That's what made all this trouble. Now, the shocks like the one we had today are caused by the earth trying to make it over the other horn! When it gets that done, there'll be no more shocks."

Captain Byrne's eyebrows were raised in disbelief. But he knew better than to argue this theory with his determined host. "Well, sir, mayhap you're right—" he was saying as he turned his head to see a woman and a small boy about five years old coming from the woods toward the blockhouse. They looked very tired, as if they'd been walking a long time. The lady was carrying a bulging carpetbag and the boy had a cloth-wrapped bundle tied with rope.

The captain got up from his seat on a log and motioned to the two boys. "Abe, you and Gus—better give that lady and her little boy some help—" and then he stopped, staring in disbelief. His face, usually ruddy, turned pale.

CHAPTER 13

All Aboard for New Orleans

Captain Byrne's voice trailed off as he stood there, staring at the newcomers.

"Yes, sir," Abe said. "Come on, Gus." But before the boys could take two steps, the captain pushed them aside, striding toward the woman. *He looks like he saw a ghost,* Abe thought. "Hold back a minute, Gus. Looks like the captain knows that lady," he said

They waited about twenty feet back. The woman, too, had turned pale. "Rita—is it really you?" they heard the captain say, and she, in turn said, "Jonathan?" and dropped the carpetbag to the ground.

And then, their gruff captain was holding the woman close and saying something the boys couldn't hear very well. The only words that came clearly were, "...Thought you were dead." The little boy, looking up at the two grown-ups, seemed as puzzled as Abe and Gus.

"They must have known each other and thought the other one had died," Gus said. "You suppose they were sweethearts once?"

"Could be." Abe's voice faded off. He was staring at the woman. As her face lost its tired, worn look, recognition came into his mind. "That's the lady in the picture!"

"Huh? What are you talkin' about?"

"Never mind. Barney said it was none of my business."

Abe had never seen so broad a smile on Captain Byrne's face as he saw now when the captain, with his arm around the woman's shoulders, turned to the boys and called. "Here, you two! Gus, take that heavy bag from the lady, and Abe, this little lad's been walking all day, so take his bundle, too. Take their things up to the blockhouse." As Abe and Gus left the little group, Captain Byrne was down on one knee reaching out to the small boy.

A few of the men and most of the women and girls, including Toni and her new friend, Madame Trudeau, were waiting at the blockhouse to greet the newcomers. Captain Byrne was fairly beaming as he brought the lady and the boy inside. Abe and Gus, having set the carpet bag and the bundle on the floor near the door, decided to stay and hear what the captain had to say.

"I want you all to meet my wife, Margarita Byrne," the captain said. "And here is my son—and I didn't even know I had one! Name's James Jonathan Byrne." Still beaming with the joy of finding his little family, he went on to explain the situation. "My wife and I haven't seen each other since I started out from Blennerhassett Island, 'way up the Ohio River, five years back—we both thought the other must be dead."

Captain Byrne couldn't seem to take his eyes off his wife and little son. He explained that he and Margarita had met in New Orleans when it was still under Spanish rule. He'd had a smaller keelboat then, and used it to take cargo down the Ohio and the lower Mississippi to New Orleans. They renewed their friendship each time the captain arrived at New Orleans for the next two years. In 1804, soon after the United States bought the big area called "Louisiana," the land that included both New Orleans and St. Louis, they were married. Margarita went with him on his voyages.

The couple had started down the Ohio from Pittsburgh on a voyage in August of 1806, and made a stop at Blennerhassett Island, just downriver from Marietta, Ohio. Mr. Harman Blennerhassett, a wealthy man from Ireland, built a fine house on that island, a mansion nothing like any of the log or simple board buildings of the nearby Ohio towns.

"We were going to have a baby and I thought it best for Rita not to go with me on that voyage," the captain said. "We had arranged for her to stay at Blennerhassett Island until I got back. She was hired to help Mrs. Blennerhassett and to be a companion to her. Mrs. Blennerhassett had taken a shine to my beautiful Rita." He turned to smile at his wife.

So he had left Rita there, early in August of 1806, promising to be back to get her at least a month before time for the baby's expected arrival in January. He didn't know that Mr. Blennerhassett was involved in a plan that got him into trouble with the government of the United States. The captain was on a hard upriver keelboat journey, when the trouble reached a climax. President Jefferson sent soldiers to arrest Blennerhassett for treason. Early in December, the Blennerhassett house was taken over by soldiers, and the Blennerhassett family and Margarita Byrne tried to escape by starting down the river in a houseboat.

"I was heading up the Ohio in the first weeks of December, a little earlier than expected," the captain explained. "Soon the ice floes would be in the river and

I needed to get my wife settled, perhaps in Marietta—in Ohio not far from Blennerhassett Island. But I got up to the island only to find the Blennerhassetts gone. Rita says she was with them as far as Louisville, in Kentucky, where this little fellow was born." He reached down to James Jonathan.

Margarita Byrne touched her husband's arm and said, "I watched for his boat for those first weeks in Louisville. All the boats have to stop to get a guide through those dangerous rocks. But I had to give up...."

"I was ahead of schedule," the captain said, "And I'm quite sure I passed the Blennerhassett boat as we worked our way back upriver. It may have been at night, because we didn't always stop—I wanted to get back to Rita as soon as possible.

"At Blennerhassett, no one could tell me where she had gone. Soldiers had taken over the beautiful house and it... I thought that she and the baby had both died—" and the captain couldn't go on for thinking of it.

When he could control his voice he said, "I stopped going up the Ohio, had the *Rosalie* built, and just worked between New Orleans and St. Louis."

"How wonderful it is that we found each other," Rita said. "I was finally heading for New Orleans to find my parents, and was on a small keelboat when the earthquake hit. It was wrecked when mud and a great tree came down on it. And look at the good that came out of that horrible experience!"

The captain said, "It's just a miracle that we finally found each other!" He turned and looked at Abe and Gus, standing near the wall. "And if you two hadn't got separated from us, we wouldn't have stopped here this long. Another good thing from the awful earthquakes!"

Toni, her father and Madame Trudeau were among those who listened in fascination to the tale of the reunion. When the story ended, the women in the blockhouse suggested that Mrs. Byrne and James should have some dinner and then rest there in the blockhouse. The Lagrandes, Mme. Trudeau, a few other women and all the men went outside, including a now grinning Captain Byrne, Gus and Abe.

Abe wanted to go to talk with Toni, but she seemed very much involved with Madame Trudeau. He and Gus were leaning against the blockhouse wall not far from where Toni and her new friend were talking, near enough to hear what Madame Trudeau was saying.

"This wonderful meeting of the captain of your boat with his lost wife and child is like a great miracle. We have been praying since all this began, *ma cherie*. Maybe that and your boat's safe arrival are answers we are receiving."

"My papa and I, we have prayed, too—for safety and for other things, Madame Trudeau."

The woman smiled and said, "Please call me Louise, dear child. Somehow, I think we are going to be friends, Antoinette, not just for tonight but for a long time."

Toni's back was toward Abe and he was sure she had not seen him standing there. He heard her say, "I would like that, Louise. And I would like you to call me Toni, like Abe does. He is my best friend on the boat."

Toni told her that Abe had been teaching her English. "He is a nice boy, but I don't like the other one—that Gus."

172

They were deep in animated conversation, sometimes in English, sometimes in French.

Abe, hearing Toni's remarks, was pleased, but realized he really shouldn't be listening. "Come on, Gus," he said, "Let's find out what damage was done to the *Rosalie*."

They walked toward the captain, and saw he was talking with Mr. Lagrande, who looked happier than usual. The boys heard him saying, "Captain, this is just what my daughter needs—to be with women and girls. She begged me to let her stay up here with them last night and I couldn't refuse her. So I went down to the boat to sleep. But after all that's been happening, I hated to let her be apart from me, and I tell you, Captain, when that earthquake shock came in the night, it was all I could do to keep from coming up here to make sure she was all right."

Captain Byrne said, "But you knew they would take good care of her—it's plain to see that they love her, too. She sure looks happy, sir. I never heard her laugh like she does with these people!"

Abe, with Gus, was still standing nearby, waiting to speak to the captain when Toni came running up and took hold of her father's sleeve. "Papa, I must talk to you," she said, and father and daughter stepped away for a private conversation. When it was finished, Toni was smiling happily, and hurried back to where Madame Trudeau waited near the blockhouse. She seemed to have good news for her friend, Abe decided, because the two laughed and hugged.

Captain Byrne turned to the waiting boys. "Abe, come on down to the *Rosalie*. You can get the cabins straightened up. I think we'll fix a bunk for my wife in the ladies' cabin for now, and my little fellow can bunk with me—if he wants to. Don't know yet if he's going to take to the boat—maybe he'll need to be with his mother—" The captain seemed a bit lost in thought.

"Yes, sir, I'll get things ready—either way," Abe said. "Is the *Rosalie* all right?"

The captain took off his cap and ran his fingers through his thinning hair. Abe was rather glad to hear one of the well known grunts before the answer to his question. "Yes and no. Things got pretty messed up again last night. All that shaking up loosened some of the planking and I want to make sure we'll have safe going on down the river. The crew will work the rest of the day. We'll plan a start early in the morning, if the *Rosalie* is in good repair."

Gus grabbed hold of the captain's sleeve. Smiling, he said, "Cap'n, thanks for these boots and this jacket."

The captain seemed a bit startled to hear Gus remembering to express gratitude. His response was what Abe expected, another grunt. The old Gus came forth with, "I guess you're glad I was around to save Abe and get the skiff back to you."

Captain Byrne grunted again. "I saw Abe pulling you out of the water—you'd jolly well better have helped him when he needed it. And it seems to me that it was because of you that we lost the skiff in the first place."

There was silence for a moment and Gus squirmed uncomfortably. Then he said, "Yes, sir." The captain started to walk toward the bluff edge to go down to the

Rosalie. Gus, undaunted, hurried after him and plucked his sleeve.

"Guess you could use another good hand on the boat in this rough water," he said.

The captain's only response was another grunt. He turned to call an order down to Barney, to be sure the skiff was taken from the water and put on the stern deck with the cargo.

Gus said, "Does that mean I can have a job?"

Abe wondered what Captain Byrne would say to that. He saw the captain's face turn redder than usual as he glared at Gus. "No. It means I might be able to use a GOOD extra hand. And as for you, we'll say goodbye and good luck. And I hope you thanked Mr. Lagrande properly for your new clothes. And see that you help the folks here any way that you can until you start back home. Understand me?"

Gus' mouth fell open. "B-b-but I thought you'd let me ride along down to New Orleans. I could help Abe."

"No. Abe doesn't need help." Captain Byrne turned on his heel and walked a few steps away from the boys. Then he turned back again, an angry glint in his eyes. "You've got a lot to learn, Gus. If you're going to get along in this world, you have to be ready to pitch in where help is needed, quit complaining, and stop blaming everyone else for your problems."

Abe wondered if Gus realized that was the same advice he'd given him. *Probably not,* he thought. *But Gus did seem a little better than he had been. Maybe he's just a little slow to catch on....* Somehow, Abe couldn't dislike his old classmate as much as he did before they'd been forced into their camping trip together.

Captain Byrne looked toward the blockhouse, seeming deep in thought. "No, I'll let them rest…" and turned back toward the bluff. "Come on, Abe. Let's see what needs to be done to make my wife and my son comfortable." There was a special sound to the captain's voice that had never been there before. He straightened his shoulders and started toward the river in long strides. "Work to do, Abe. Let's get ready to go to New Orleans!"

Gus was left standing alone.

Mr. Lagrande was hurrying to catch up to the captain as he and Abe started down the bluff to the river. "Captain Byrne," Lagrande called, and the captain turned. "May I speak to you before you go down to the boat?" As the captain came back a few steps, the Frenchman went on, "My Toni has a special request. I know your wonderful fortune in finding your wife and son means they'll need space on the *Rosalie,* but I still must ask. May we take on another passenger for the ladies' cabin, Captain? I'd like to pay Madame Trudeau's fare to New Orleans, so that there will be a companion for my daughter."

Captain Byrne saw no objection to the plan. "We have four bunks in the ladies' cabin and so far just two or three are spoken for. Tell Mme. Trudeau she may go with us, of course. I'm sure my Rita will also be glad to have her company."

He said to Abe a minute later. "We'll have a full house now, all the way to New Orleans. Going to keep you busy, Abe, pleasing all those women-folk!"

176

"Don't mind at all," Abe said. "And I don't think Toni will be lonesome any more!"

"Then let's get to work to make our ladies comfortable."

Abe grinned. "Aye, aye, sir!" he said.

When the other blockhouse people heard that Louise Trudeau, the only woman there without another family member, was going to be leaving on the *Rosalie,* they gathered around her for farewells.

"I wish we all could go. It is so frightening since the earthquake came," one said.

"Any chance of that, Captain Byrne?" a man asked.

"Sorry, ladies and gentlemen," he replied. "My *Rosalie* has a full roster now. We are already heavily loaded. But surely you are now through the worst of this earthquake problem, and will be finding a way to rebuild your homes soon.

"By the way, I'm leaving that big young fellow—Gus— here. He's never been much good, but I think he might be a better young man if he works to help you. I hope you'll give him a chance, anyway. He's got a lot to learn and it will sure be good for him."

Gus seemed to brighten up as he heard one of the men answer the captain. "Well, sir, I for one know I'll need all the help I can get when I go back to try to rebuild my cabin. I can use the help of a strong young fellow." The man's wife nodded assent and turned and smiled at Gus. Gus seemed almost to beam in response.

"Just let me know what you want me to do," he said. "I'm your man!"

With the first light of morning, it was time for the *Rosalie* to get underway. Many of the blockhouse people were out to watch the departure of their new friends. As the captain reached his post on the cabin roof and picked up the long rudder pole, he waved and called back, "My men and my little family and I thank you for your hospitality, and wish you Godspeed to better days."

The five passengers were on board, all out on the deck waving. Toni, standing with Madame Trudeau beside her, looked more happy and excited than she had been since the *Rosalie* began her downstream voyage. The lines were pulled in. As the *Rosalie* moved out of her mooring and into the snag-clogged Mississippi, the people of the blockhouse waved a last goodbye.

Abe was sent to check the cargo on the stern deck to make sure it was secure. As the keelboat headed down the Mississippi once again, he paused for one last look at the little fort on the bluff and the group of new friends watching the departure. Gus was standing alongside the man who had spoken for his help. To Abe, he looked as if he had grown an inch taller overnight, and he wondered if it would be a "new" Gus he'd see when they were both back in St. Louis.

Then, shrugging his shoulders, Abe began to whistle a happy tune as he went about his work.

Postlude

Abe's Letter Home

New Orleans

January 16, 1812

Dear Mama and Papa, and Hannah and Rachel,

I hope all of you are well and that our house did not fall down in the earthquakes. I do not know if St. Louis felt it very much, but it sure was bad on the boat. You will be glad to know that I am all right and at Uncle Daniel and Aunt Mattie's house.

Mama, you were right about feeling that something bad might happen. It did. We were just one day south of New Madrid when the earthquakes started in the middle of the night, right in the worst part of the river. It sure was scary!!! The captain had moored the boat in a good place, everyone said, at a sloping bank and not right under a bluff where the whole thing might have fallen on us. But I was really scared. I tried not to show it too much. Especially around Toni. Remember her? She was the pretty girl who spoke French and was staying at the Chouteau house. I like her very much and she likes me, too. She will be going back to St. Louis to live, so we can keep on being friends. Sure glad we had such a good crew, too. I liked the captain and Barney, the first mate, real well.

Down here in New Orleans we hardly feel the earthquake shocks, but Uncle Daniel read in the newspaper that they are still going on up near New Madrid. He says there's hardly anything left of that town and that lots of people's homes are gone. We met some nice people farther down the river at an old fort on a bluff. They were all too scared to stay at their houses, and some of their houses had fallen apart or gone sliding away from where they were supposed to be.

Our boat got into New Orleans just yesterday. We were on the river for 39 days. I took Mama's letter to Uncle Daniel's house as soon as I could find out where it was. He and Aunt Mattie were so surprised to see me! I think they were kind of glad, too. I guess they thought I was just a little boy, like I was that time they came to St. Louis. They have a little room for me to use while I am here. They gave me this paper and ink and a pen to write to you.

Hannah and Rachel, Toni wants to get to know you when she gets back to St. Louis. Oh—you will remember that big bully named Gus. He was on a flatboat that got wrecked in the earthquake. He came along the river holding onto a log and bumped into our skiff at the back of the Rosalie. We had an awful adventure together when we were both in the skiff and it got pulled away from the big boat. The Mississippi really was WILD. I will tell you all about it when I'm back home. But I think maybe Gus will be a nicer guy when he gets back to St. Louis. We left him with the people at the old fort. I don't know if he stayed long or started for home. Maybe he's back in St. Louis already. I feel kind of sorry for him.

Toni was lonesome because her mama died last year. But a French lady who was at the fort was lonesome, too. Her husband and her little girl were killed in a fire. She came the rest of the way to

New Orleans with us. Now she and Toni and Toni's papa are all good friends.

And the captain was lonesome too, but he had a big surprise when we were at the old fort. He thought his wife had died five years ago, but she was still alive and came to the fort while we were there. And they have a little boy. Now they are here in New Orleans and the captain is planning that they will have a home in St. Louis, too. He used to just grunt instead of saying something, but I haven't heard him grunt like that for all the time since we left the fort.

Papa, when we were about half way to Natchez, that big steamboat *New Orleans* that we read about in the newspaper, caught up with us. It left us behind in no time! But it sure made a lot of black smoke and noise! I wish you could have seen it.

I am too sleepy to write any more now.

January 28, 1812

No boat was starting up the river to take my letter to you, and I'm glad. They would have gone into more earthquakes. I was reading the newspaper here and it said there was another real bad one up there just five days ago, on January 23. I hope that's the last one! I wish I could find out if you are all right. The paper said that this quake was even worse than the first one. And that one was terrible. I hope they end soon. It would be awful to have another one on the way home. But Mama, don't start worrying about me again.

The captain says I can go back with the *Rosalie*. There'll be lots of work for a cabin boy, because there will be five passengers to take care of. He says the river should be open by the time we get up north if we start about the 10th of February, but it will be a slow trip because the earthquakes have changed the riverbed so much. Barney will have to really watch for a channel. His little guide book won't be any help now. Maybe I can help him see the dangerous places. He taught me a lot about how to see underwater snags. Captain Byrne says I should be home, if the weather is good, about the middle of April. I can hardly wait!

Toni and her father will be on the boat too—and I kind of think Madame Trudeau will be along with them. I think she's going to be Toni's new mama. You will like them and Mrs. Byrne, too. She's a Spanish lady who is really American now.

Captain's real anxious to get away from New Orleans, because people keep talking about how the English navy ships will be coming to try to capture this city. The kegs of shot we brought down are stored to help the people defend New Orleans. So far there's no sign of the battle happening, but I read in Uncle Daniel's newspaper about people being sure a war is going to start.

I think I told you about finding a piece of paper in the captain's cabin that first day he asked me to help him, before we started on this trip. It was stuck in the boards, and he didn't want me to know what it was. Well, now I know. I'll tell you about it when I'm home. It meant Captain Byrne might be in trouble with the government. So right away Captain Byrne is going to get it fixed. He went to see a lawyer here in New Orleans who says he can take care of it. I'm glad of that because Captain Byrne is such a good man and he doesn't need anything more to worry about. I'm even gladder that he found his wife and little boy.

I wish that steamboat could take me back home, but the *New Orleans* got stuck at Natchez where the current in the river gets bad, so she just goes on trips between Natchez and New Orleans. Captain Byrne says some day soon there will be a steamboat going all the way, that there are other steamboats being built now that are different with stronger steam engines. He wants to be captain on a steamboat because it's awfully hard for the boatmen to get a loaded keelboat up the river. Takes a long time, too, and the steamboat *New Orleans* can go up to Natchez a lot faster than a keelboat.

Papa, I know now that I don't want to be a boatman—unless I get a job on a steamboat. It's such hard work for the men and I know it will be very slow going back up the Mississippi to get me back home.

I've been doing some bookkeeping for Captain Byrne and for Uncle Daniel, too. That's all right, but I don't think it's what I really want to do. I went on an errand for the captain to his lawyer's office here, and the lawyer was really helping the captain get things straightened out. So if Colonel Easton didn't find another boy to study law with him, please tell him I'd like to talk to him about it. And, Papa, tell him I am really glad he had me write out those lines. I say them often and they help me decide what I should do—like when Gus was going to drown if I didn't rescue him. That line—to thine own self be true—is the best.

Maybe when I'm a lawyer I can take all of you to Washington. We could go as far as Pittsburgh on one of those new steamboats!

Mama, I bought new boots here, like you told me to. They are bigger than my old ones. Guess I'm finally growing, 'cause my pants are all too short. Aunt Mattie is going to help me get some new ones. I am earning enough money to pay for them.

I just found out that the *New Orleans* is going up to Natchez this week and this letter can go that far on the steamboat. From there I hope there will be post riders to take it farther and maybe you'll get it before we start back up the river on the *Rosalie*. Please tell Towser I miss him, too, and give him a bone for me.

Your loving son and brother,

Abraham Benjamin Carson

P.S. My voice doesn't squeak as much as it used to do.